Something's watching Meg . . .

The fountain was splashing merrily in the sunshine as I walked down the brick path. I paused beside the statue again. It couldn't possibly be as scary as I'd remembered, could it?

Yes, I realized with a jolt as I took it in again. *It could be.* How could anyone have chosen such a hideous creature to stand in front of their house?

Not only did the statue look just as frightening, it appeared to have moved since I'd last seen it. Hadn't the statue's head been pointing *away* from the front door when Pittsy and I had arrived? Why was it staring *toward* the front door now, as if it were waiting for me?

I shuddered and took off down the path. Obviously my imagination was still out of control. I didn't let myself glance back.

But as I got onto my bike and pedaled away, I couldn't escape the feeling that the statue was watching me leave.

Books by Ann Hodgman

My Babysitter Is a Vampire
My Babysitter Has Fangs
My Babysitter Bites Again

Coming Soon

Stinky Stanley

Available from MINSTREL Books

My Babysitter Bites Again

by
Ann Hodgman

Illustrated by
John Pierard

A GLC Book

PUBLISHED BY POCKET BOOKS
New York London Toronto Sydney Tokyo Singapore

In memory of Kathie Isselee,
who had a way with all kinds of babies

A MINSTREL PAPERBACK *ORIGINAL*

A Minstrel Book published by
POCKET BOOKS, a division of Simon & Schuster Inc.
1230 Avenue of the Americas, New York, NY 10020

Special thanks to Ruth Ashby and Pat MacDonald.

Cover painting by Jeffrey Lindberg
Illustrations by John Pierard
Typesetting by Jackson Typesetting
Developed by Byron Preiss and Daniel Weiss
Edited by Lisa Meltzer

ISBN: 0-671-79378-0

First Minstrel Books printing July 1993
10 9 8 7 6 5 4 3 2 1

Printed in the U.S.A.

My Babysitter Bites Again

CHAPTER ONE

"I mean, I really *need* more allowance to take my mind off my tragedy," Kelly Pitts told me in a gloomy voice. "Right now my parents are practically *starving* me."

I sighed. Kelly and I had been sitting on the beach for an hour. The Atlantic Ocean was glistening blue, the air was warm and crisp at the same time, the breeze smelled of salt and sunscreen. It was a beautiful beach day—and I had to spend it listening to Kelly talk about her tiny allowance.

Actually, Kelly Pitts's allowance is twice the size of mine. No way is she starving. And, actually, I don't call her Kelly—I call her Pittsy. She doesn't know that, of course, and I try not to let it slip out.

My name is Meg Swain. I'm twelve years old and going into seventh grade. The beach where I was sitting with Pittsy was on Moose Island, a little island off the coast of Maine where my family spends every summer. It was Pittsy's first summer there. Her house was down the beach from mine, which meant that I was stuck being friends with her whether I liked it or not.

So far, Pittsy had had an exciting summer falling in love with a vampire who used to babysit for me. I'll fill you in on that later. Luckily for her, the romance hadn't worked out. Unluckily for me, Pittsy still wasn't over it.

"You wouldn't understand, Meg, because you're so totally much younger than I am," she said, fluffing out her long blond hair importantly. (Pittsy is fourteen—very, very impressive, as far as she's concerned.) "But with all that's happened to me this summer, I need *distractions.* I need to amuse myself so I won't keep *thinking* about things." She rolled onto her stomach and began inspecting her fingernails, each of which had a different color of nail polish. "And to do all that, I need *way* more money than my stupid parents are willing to—"

"A-ba-ba-ba-ba-BAH!" someone interrupted.

Someone who really *was* totally much younger than Pittsy—about thirteen years younger, maybe? And quite a lot cuter, too. He was a little, round, wiggly baby whose parents had just spread out a towel next to ours and plopped him down on it. While they scrambled to set up their stuff—people with babies always have about fifty times more beach stuff than ordinary people, I've noticed—the baby sat still for a second, looking around. Then he pushed himself to his feet and toddled over to the edge of his towel.

"A-ba-ba-ba-ba-BAH!" he repeated, smiling at me.

"Hi there," I answered, smiling back. It was impossible not to smile at this baby. He had fuzzy, stick-uppy black hair and bright black eyes. His tummy stuck out so far that I figured his miniature red bathing suit had only about a five percent chance of staying up. As I watched, he bent over, picked up a handful of sand, and carefully dropped it onto my knee.

"Thanks," I said gravely.

Pittsy wasn't paying attention to any of this. I guess studying her fingernails had exhausted her. She yawned and pulled a towel over her head as she rolled onto her back again.

The baby's mother, who was slim and expensive looking, glanced over at him adoringly. "Are you flirting, Vaughnie?" she asked. To me, she said, "He's very friendly."

"Yes, I can see that," I answered, ducking as the baby tried to pat my eyes with his sandy hand. "How old is he?"

"He had his first birthday last week. He's big for his age, isn't he?" his mother said proudly.

I really don't know about baby sizes, so I just nodded. At that point the baby picked up a little sand shovel and started whacking my legs with it.

"Uh-oh," I said. Gently I lifted the shovel out of his hand and put it down on the towel. "No hitting, honey!"

"No, no, that's okay!" said his mother quickly. "It's no problem. You can let him have the shovel. That's a *shovel,* Vaughn," she said. "Can you say *shovel*?"

I was a little surprised. I mean, I knew the baby wasn't trying to hurt me. He just felt like whacking something with a shovel, and my legs happened to be convenient. Still, they were *my* legs. Most parents don't let their kids go around hitting other people. It's their job to train them out of stuff like that.

"Buh-*ga,*" said the baby.

His mother beamed at him. "You said it! You said it!" She turned excitedly to her husband, who was struggling to stick a beach umbrella into the sand. "Steve, the baby said *shovel*!"

Her husband let the beach umbrella fall to the sand—he was lucky it didn't hit anyone!—and rushed over to his son. "Vaughn, that's super!" he crowed. "Your first word!"

"Buh-ga-ga-ga-ga-ga-ga-ga-ga-ga-ga-ga," Vaughn replied.

It didn't sound much like *shovel* to me, but why argue? If it made them happy . . . Parents probably always acted like that with their first babies. My parents had probably acted like that with me.

Still, as the afternoon went on, I wondered if maybe these parents were giving in to Vaughn a little *too* much. No matter how cute he was, weren't there supposed to be some rules?

Whenever Vaughn even looked at the ocean, one of his parents would pick him up and rush him over to the water. Whenever he even brushed against their picnic basket, they would coo, "Snackie? Juice-y?" and open the basket for him.

They let him drop food in the sand and then feed it to them.

They let him take off their sunglasses and step on them.

They let him grab my sunscreen and squeeze it out all over my towel.

"Isn't that *sweet*?" his mother said to me. "He wants to keep you from getting a sunburn!"

I kind of half smiled. Vaughn was such a giggly, cute baby that I couldn't be mad at him. But I was definitely starting to think that it might be time to go home.

Then Vaughn's mother spoke up. "We haven't

introduced ourselves, have we? I'm Wendy Grimm, and this is my husband, Steve."

Pittsy and I told them our names—me politely, Pittsy sleepily, from under her towel. (She called herself Kelly, of course.)

"Do you live on the island year-round?" Mrs. Grimm asked.

We explained how I had been coming here summers forever but that this was Pittsy's first.

"It's our first time here too," Mrs. Grimm said. "We just bought a house on Spider Point."

Spider Point isn't too far from the part of the island where Pittsy and I live—but it's a lot fancier. The houses there are *huge.* At the turn of the century, rich families along with packs of servants used to come to Spider Point for the whole summer. I always imagine the poor servants staggering around in the hot sun with these huge trunks on their backs.

"We're hoping to have the place fixed up enough to spend the whole summer here next year," Mr. Grimm explained. "But this year we're just spending three weeks."

"So Vaughn can have his first ocean experience," his wife put in. "And speaking of Vaughn, you two don't happen to know any babysitters, do you? I'd love to get out without him once in a while. Just so I don't have to drag him along on a lot of boring errands," she added hastily, as if she was afraid we'd think she was a bad mother.

Before I could even open my mouth, Pittsy had yanked the towel off her head and sat up. All of a sudden she didn't look sleepy anymore.

"*I'm* a very experienced babysitter," she said quickly. "I've had lots of—you know—child-care experience back home."

This was news to me. As far as I could tell, Pittsy hardly knew the difference between a baby and a bottle of ketchup. But she kept right on talking.

"I just adore little babies," she crooned, chucking Vaughn clumsily under his chin. (He looked startled and turned away. Maybe he wasn't used to such long fingernails.) "And he is, like, so adorable! When would you like me to start? I'm free all the time."

I thought Mrs. Grimm looked a little startled, too. "Well, that's—that's a nice offer, Kelly," she said. "Maybe we could try an hour or so at first, just to see how it goes."

"Great," said Pittsy eagerly. "I'll give you my number. Wait a minute." She turned to me. "Do you have a piece of paper, Meg?"

"Nope. Sorry," I said shortly. "I've got to get going, anyway."

I didn't feel like sticking around and watching Pittsy get a babysitting job that *I* wanted—just because *she* wanted money. True, she had spoken up before I did. But it still didn't seem fair.

"I've got some paper in my beach bag somewhere," said Mrs. Grimm. She reached into the bag and began rummaging through millions of diapers and bottles of juice. At last she pulled out a crumpled shred of newspaper and a felt-tip pen without a cap. "Here you go."

I gathered up my stuff and stood up to leave. "See you around, everyone," I said.

Pittsy and the Grimms barely raised their heads, but the baby gave me a little wave. "Dadoy," he said. Maybe that meant "bye-bye."

I stalked toward the path that led to the bike racks, where I'd locked my bike. Halfway there I glanced back.

What I saw chilled me to the bone.

Pittsy had picked up Vaughn and was bouncing him on her knee. There was nothing wrong with that, of course, except for her expression. As she looked down at him, she looked almost—almost hungry. She might have been staring at a candy store window instead of at a child.

The breeze must have been blowing toward me because I heard her words very clearly.

"He's so sweet," she was saying. "Really, I could just eat him up."

I know people use that expression all the time, but Pittsy looked as though she really *did* wish she could eat Vaughn up.

And considering that Pittsy might be a vampire, that wasn't the way I wanted her looking at a helpless little baby.

CHAPTER TWO

I'd better explain a few things. Not that my explanation will make much sense, and not that you'll believe me. In fact, you'd be crazy to believe me. But what I'm about to tell you is the truth anyway.

Last summer my little brother, Trevor, and I had a teenage vampire for a babysitter. His name was Vincent Graver, and he also worked at the blood bank in the same medical center as my mother. (She's a medical student.) Mom thought Vincent was such a polite boy—and she was so frantically busy—that she hired him to take care of us without even noticing that he had pointed teeth and a complexion like a dead fish.

Naturally Trevor and I didn't like having a vampire take care of us. I mean, most babysitters don't drink blood out of a portable flask! Trevvie was too little to do much, but I managed to get rid of Vincent with the help of my friend Jack Cornell, who's a year older than I am and lives on Moose Island year-round.

Unfortunately, it turned out that Vincent wasn't gone for good. Vampires are harder to get rid of than I had realized, and Vincent turned up again *this* summer.

Not as a babysitter this time, of course. I'm old enough to sit for Trevor myself now. This time around, Vincent was careful not to let me or Jack see him. Instead, he made friends with Pittsy. He even tricked her into thinking that he was in love with her—the poor dope. (Pittsy, I mean.) So when Jack and I found out he was still around, we had to get rid of him *again.* It would take too long to describe how we did it. But considering that Vincent ended up as a pile of ashes that we buried at sea, I really didn't think we'd be running into him again.

That still left Pittsy, though, and sometimes I worried about her. Vincent had bitten her neck a couple of times while he was pretending to kiss her. ("I wonder—which is grosser?" Jack once asked. "Being bitten by a vampire, or being kissed by one?") Exactly how *many* bites Vincent had given her I didn't know.

If it was just one or two, I knew Pittsy would be okay. If a vampire bites you three times, though, you become a vampire yourself.

The problem was that Pittsy didn't remember how many times Vincent had bitten her. "He kissed me three times, and it sure *felt* like bites," she had told me and Jack. "But maybe that was just part of his, you know, personal technique." Since neither Jack nor I especially felt like talking about vampires' "personal techniques," we had dropped the subject. But once or twice I'd wondered if Pittsy's teeth weren't starting to look a little pointy. . . .

Anyway, now you can see why I wasn't too comfortable when I saw Pittsy staring greedily at little Vaughn. What was she greedy *for*—money or blood?

I sighed as I biked home from the beach. Jack couldn't help me out this time. A week before he had enrolled in an all-day sailing program that was going to last for the rest of the summer. "I've done enough vampire stuff," he said. "Now I just want to do sailing stuff."

Thanks a lot, Jack, I thought now. *You deserter. And thanks a lot, Pittsy. You job-stealer.*

The rest of the summer looked as though it was going to be a total loss.

Not that I had liked having Vincent around. But at least he made things more interesting. At least being scared all the time kept me from dozing off, unlike being bored all the time.

At least fighting off vampires was something to do.

* * *

When I got home from the beach, I fed our cat, Pooch, and then moped around for a couple of hours until suppertime. I would have moped at supper, too, except that I didn't get a chance.

"I bet there are onions in that meat loaf, right?" Trevor asked my mother gloomily as she started filling his plate. "Lots and lots of horrible slimy onions."

"No more than usual," said my mother calmly. Turning to my father, she asked how his day had gone.

Dad is a screenwriter, which means he writes movie scripts. He wasn't actually writing a script right then—just planning one. (He calls it "working on a treatment.") As far as I could see, the only work he ever did was talk on the phone and rent movies. "For research," he always said when we'd catch him watching some awful old garbagey cop movie. "I need to soak up the atmosphere."

"My day was fine," Dad said now. "I was on the phone all morning. I had lunch at the Buttery." The Buttery is a gourmet shop in town. "Then I spent the afternoon on the phone."

"Sounds stressful," said Mom dryly. She didn't really have much to complain about, though. Last summer Mom had been crazy with all her work at the medical center. This summer her only job was to write up the results of some experiments she had done over the winter.

"*I* had a terrible day, if anyone is interested," I said. "I was on the beach with Pittsy, and—"

"Well, *I* had an even *terribler* day," Trevor interrupted me. "Can't we go back home? I hate it here!"

"You hate Moose Island?" Mom looked surprised. "I thought you were having fun!"

"I was," said Trevor grumpily. "But now people keep following me around."

Both my parents looked surprised now. "Following you?" Dad repeated. "What do you mean, Trev?"

"*You* know." Trevor gave his meat loaf a moody poke with his fork. "Like watching me and breathing on me and stuff."

"But, honey, you were in the house with me all day!" Mom said. "*I* certainly wasn't following you around."

Trevor seemed puzzled. "No," he agreed. "But someone was. When I was up in my room, I could feel eyes staring at me." Suddenly his chin began to tremble. "So that's why I want to go home," he said in a wobbly voice. "I don't like those eyes."

My parents gave each other a quick glance. This wasn't like Trevor. He's got a great imagination, but he doesn't imagine *eyes* staring at him.

"I'm sorry you're so worried and upset, Trevor," said Dad at last. "Mom and I will try to help you feel better. But we're not leaving Moose Island until the end of the summer—and you know that's still a few weeks off."

Trevor's eyes filled with tears. "It's not fair," he choked out.

"Well, I guess it doesn't seem fair," Dad agreed. "But that's the way we have to do it."

Trevor gave a gusty sigh and changed the subject. "You *know* I hate onions, Mom," he said, jabbing fiercely at his meat loaf. "So can I give my meat loaf to Pooch?"

"You've got to help me, Meg," Pittsy begged desperately. It was the next morning, and she had woken me out of a sound sleep (okay, I had been reading, but I was still in bed) to call me on the phone.

"They want me to come over right now!" she wailed.

"Who do?" I asked.

"The Gramms. Grimms, I mean. They want me to come over to see them, like, right away!"

"Isn't that what you wanted?" I said coldly.

"No! I mean yes! I mean, I want the job, but *I* don't know anything about little kids!"

She didn't have to tell me that, but I was at

least glad she was admitting it. "Then why did you take the—"

"Job?" Pittsy finished for me. "Because I really *need* a job! I've got to have more money to take my *mind* off my—"

"It's okay," I cut in hastily. "I remember."

"So, anyway, I told them you were coming with me," Pittsy said abruptly.

"What?"

"To get introduced to their house in case I ever need a substitute, I told them. I hope you don't mind."

"I *do* mind!" I gave my own ponytail a yank, I was so mad. "You just want me to cover for you so the Grimms won't know what a know-nothing you are!"

"That's a nice thing to say to someone who's so much older than you," Pittsy said with dignity. Then she must have remembered that she was supposed to be buttering me up. "Anyway, Meg, can't you help me out this once?" Then she must have forgotten again. "I'm sure you don't have anything better to do," she added.

Amazingly enough, I ended up going along with her. Why? Well, partly because I'm such a pushover. And partly because I had never been inside any of the houses at Spider Point, and this might be my only chance.

And partly because Pittsy was right. I *didn't* have anything better to do.

As we climbed off our bikes, Pittsy checked the address she had written down the day before. "This is it," she said. "The Gramms' house. Grimms', I mean. Wow, it's kind of—uh—big, isn't it?"

Her voice faltered a little on the word *big,* and I could see why. The Grimms' house wasn't just big. It was mammoth. And it wasn't just a mammoth *house.* It was a mammoth *ruined* house.

A huge hulk of a place, it towered over us like a tombstone in a giants' graveyard. It was made of dark gray stone and covered with snakey tendrils of ivy that twisted across the windows and dripped down from the balcony on the second floor. The brick path to the door was hemmed in on either side by tall, unkempt boxwood hedges. The front door had a round iron ring for a knocker and a tiny iron-barred window in the center. And in front of the house—

"What is that thing?" Pittsy whispered in amazement.

"A fountain," I whispered back.

"Yeah, I can see that! I mean, what's that thing in the *middle* of the fountain?"

"Some kind of statue, I guess," I said uncertainly.

Some kind of eight-foot statue with a hideous, leering face and outstretched claws that seemed poised to grab anyone who came too close. And feet that looked like dragon's claws. And a forked tail.

The water splashing playfully around the foot of the statue seemed totally out of place. It was much too clean and clear and innocent looking. *It should be molten lead,* I found myself thinking. *Or blood.*

"They sure had weird taste in the olden days," Pittsy said, shaking her head. "Why put in a fountain when you could put in a swimming pool instead? No one gets a tan at a *fountain.*"

That wasn't my problem with the fountain, but I didn't answer. I was concentrating too hard on not running away. Pittsy and I were heading up the crumbling brick path now, and every step we took toward that massive front door frightened me more.

You're just being sensitive, I tried to scold myself. *You're worse than Dad about soaking up atmosphere. You'd think you had never seen a door before! It's lucky you* didn't *get this babysitting job if you're going to be such a—*

With a shrill, eerie shriek, the front door was suddenly thrown open.

CHAPTER THREE

"Hi, girls!" Mrs. Grimm said brightly.

I was so relieved I almost collapsed. During that short walk up the path, I had managed to convince myself that some horrible, formless evil would be waiting for us behind the door. All there was, though, was Mrs. Grimm, leaning against the doorjamb in exercise clothes holding Vaughn on one hip.

"Gah-dun!" he greeted us.

Mrs. Grimm's eyes widened. "I think he recognizes you," she said in amazement. "Isn't that great? Come on in. I'll show you around. I was just about to get Vaughnie dressed."

"The place is a bit of a wreck," she went on over her shoulder as she led us into the house. "I'm sorry you have to see it this way. When it's all done it'll be gorgeous, but that won't be until next summer. Just try to pick your way over all this rubble."

The inside of the house was even creepier than

the outside, if that was possible—kind of a cross between a haunted castle and an abandoned basement. There weren't *quite* cobwebs in the corners and bats swooping down in our faces, but almost.

"The realtor told us that the man who built this house was the son of a European count and countess," Mrs. Grimm went on as we followed her through the dank central hall. It was lit with what seemed to be torches set into the walls. "*They* must have felt at home here, at least. Oh, hi, honey."

Mr. Grimm was in a dark little den off the hallway, fiddling with the cable box on a widescreen TV set. ("Thank heaven they've got cable," Pittsy whispered in my ear.)

"I can't seem to get PBS," he complained to his wife. "I guess I'll have to call the cable guys again."

"Yes, you'd better," Mrs. Grimm agreed. "Vaughnie *needs* his 'Sesame Street'! Don't you, sugar?" She dropped a kiss on the baby's head. Then she led us up an echoing stone stairwell and into the baby's room.

I could tell that the Grimms had worked hard to make this room more cheerful than the rest of the house. They'd kind of gone overboard, though. It looked as if they'd moved in an entire toy store—the kind that *my* parents always say is too expensive to shop in. A carved wooden rocking horse with a fluffy mane and tail stood at attention in one corner. A full-size toy lamb with real wool was standing in the opposite corner. One entire wall was lined with hardcover books, and none of them had the beat-up, chewed-on look of most babies' books. A drive-around electric fire engine was parked under the crib. And the crib itself was bristling so with mobiles and mirrors and busy boxes and squeak toys that there was hardly room to get the baby into it.

"We like Vaughnie to have lots of stimulation," Mrs. Grimm told us unnecessarily. She laid the baby on his changing table—which was covered with what looked like an antique baby quilt—and turned to Pittsy.

"Kelly, wouldn't you like to get the baby dressed?" she asked. "That way he can interact with you a little bit."

Pittsy gave me one stricken, terrified look. "D-dress him?" she squeaked. "What *in*?"

"We like to let him pick his own clothes," said Mrs. Grimm. She pointed to the bureau next to the changing table. "You can just pull a few things out of there and see what he feels like today."

Pittsy walked frozenly over to the bureau,

opened the top drawer (I wasn't surprised to see that it was crammed with neatly folded new clothes), and pulled out a little sweatsuit with a pattern of beach toys on it. "How about this?" she asked Mrs. Grimm.

"Don't ask *me,*" said Mrs. Grimm gaily. "Show it to Vaughn and see what *he* thinks."

Pittsy turned and tentatively held out the suit to the baby. "Um, what do you think of this, Vaughn?" she asked.

I think she actually expected Vaughn to answer. But he just lay there, staring at the ceiling and kicking his fat little feet.

"I guess that one doesn't interest him," said Mrs. Grimm. "Why don't you try something else?"

This time Pittsy took out a little hat and a red playsuit. Vaughn grabbed the hat but left the playsuit alone.

"Well, that's a good start," said Mrs. Grimm encouragingly. "Why don't you try standing him up next to the bureau to see what else he'd like to pick?"

"Pick—pick him up?" Pittsy sounded startled. "Won't he—uh—feel shy to have a stranger touching him? Maybe you'd better do it, Mrs. Grimm. Or Meg."

"He doesn't know Meg any better than he

knows you," Mrs. Grimm pointed out. "No, go ahead. Vaughnie's a very friendly baby. Aren't you, biscuit?" she cooed.

Pittsy gave me another worried glance, then picked up the baby around his waist. Holding him out stiffly in front of her—as though he were a vase of flowers she was afraid might spill—she moved him over to the bureau and stood him up in front of the drawers.

Vaughn gurgled happily and plunged his hands into the piles of clothes. The first thing he pulled out was another sun hat.

"I guess he's in a hat mood today," said Mrs. Grimm proudly. "Well, we'll figure out some way to let him wear both of them."

All three of them, she should have said. Vaughn pulled out another sun hat next and then an undershirt. Then he lost interest and starting throwing clothes on the floor.

"Which hat should I—I mean you—put on him?" asked Pittsy. "He can't wear all three of them at once."

"Oh, no! We have to let him!" said Mrs. Grimm quickly. "It wouldn't be fair to Vaughn not to honor his choices. Most parents don't give babies enough credit. Babies *always* know what they want."

Okay, I'm not a parent, but I thought that was

a pretty ridiculous theory. Wouldn't Vaughn forget about the extra hats once they were out of sight? If *I* had been the mother of a one-year-old, I would have just picked his clothes for him. I couldn't believe Vaughn really cared what he wore.

But Mrs. Grimm told Pittsy to put one hat on Vaughn's head and to stuff the other two into his socks. Then Pittsy put on his undershirt. She did it as gingerly as if she were dressing a skunk, but Mrs. Grimm didn't notice because I was distracting her with questions.

"Do you let Vaughn pick his own foods, too?" I asked.

"Of course. Leave it up to a baby, and he'll choose a well-balanced meal *every* time. All we do is make sure we're giving him good, healthy foods to choose from."

So when we were downstairs, she piled about twenty choices on Vaughn's high-chair tray and let him plow into them. They were all things like cottage cheese and mashed strawberries and grated carrots and spaghetti with tomato sauce—good, healthy foods that also happened to be incredibly messy. Vaughn rubbed most of them into his hair, but a little at least got sort of near his mouth.

Pittsy was watching in fascinated horror. "How do you clean all that stuff off?" she asked.

"Oh, I'll tell you what to do and let you do it," said Mrs. Grimm with a merry laugh. "I have to confess it will be a bit of a relief to have someone help me with *that* part."

"Meg should learn, too," said Pittsy quickly. "She might have to substitute for me sometime."

"We'll just let Meg watch for now," said Mrs. Grimm. "I don't want to confuse Vaughnie today. After all, you're going to be his first babysitter on the island."

I thought Pittsy was going to faint when she actually had to touch the baby's food shampoo. When she'd finally gotten the last of it out of his hair—she had used almost a whole roll of paper towels—she stared pleadingly at Mrs. Grimm. "I think you've shown me enough for one day, haven't you?" she asked.

"Just one more thing," said Mrs. Grimm. "Let's go back up to Vaughn's room and get his diaper changed." She wrinkled her nose. "I'm sure he *needs* a change by now."

"Wow, look at the time!" I said quickly. "I didn't realize it was so late! Pi—uh, Kelly, I'll see you tomorrow, okay?"

I jumped to my feet. "Thanks, Mrs. Grimm," I said. "I'll see you soon, I hope."

"I hope so, Meg," she answered. As I walked out of the kitchen, I heard her saying, "Now,

Kelly, why don't you take the baby out of his high chair? Oops, I guess that diaper's a little leaky, isn't it? Well, we can clean you up later."

Poor Pittsy. What an education she was turning out to get. I almost felt as if she *deserved* the money she would make with Vaughn.

I pulled open the heavy front door, stepped outside, and fell onto my face. I had tripped over something on the top step.

Rubbing my nose, I picked up the object. It was a small package wrapped in a frilly paper. On it were written—in spiky, ornate script—the words *For Dear Baby.*

Another toy, probably. Maybe someone was dropping off a late birthday present—as if Vaughn needed another toy.

I put the package on the little table in the Grimms' front hall and headed back outside again.

The fountain was splashing merrily in the sunshine as I walked down the brick path. I paused beside the statue again. It couldn't possibly be as scary as I'd remembered, could it?

Yes, I realized with a jolt as I took it in again. *It could be.* How could anyone have chosen such a hideous creature to stand in front of their house?

Not only did the statue look just as frightening,

it appeared to have moved since I'd last seen it. Hadn't the statue's head been pointing *away* from the front door when Pittsy and I had arrived? Why was it staring *toward* the front door now, as if it were waiting for me?

I shuddered and took off down the path. Obviously my imagination was still out of control. I didn't let myself glance back.

But as I got onto my bike and pedaled away, I couldn't escape the feeling that the statue was watching me leave.

CHAPTER FOUR

My brother screamed.

I sat bolt upright in bed, my heart hammering. It was after midnight, and I had been sound asleep when Trevor's shriek ripped through the air.

He screamed again. "He's here! He's here!" he cried. "No! Don't take me!"

Feet thudded across the floor, and I heard Trevor's door burst open. In a second Mom was in there speaking soothingly to him.

I couldn't hear what Trevor sobbed in reply, but Mom kept her voice calm and low. In a few minutes Trevor had settled down again. I heard my mother quietly close his door and walk back to her room.

The night turned peaceful again, but for a long time I couldn't get back to sleep.

At breakfast the next morning Trevor didn't remember anything about waking up in the middle of the night. But he was listless and pale and wouldn't eat much. My parents kept checking him out when he wasn't watching.

"I don't like the cereal they have on Moose Island," Trevor suddenly announced. "I only like the cereal we get at home."

"Trevor, it's the exact same kind!" I objected.

"No, it's not." Trevor sighed. "They took out all the good stuff."

Mom broke in before I could protest again. "Trevvie, I'd love to take you to the playground this morning," she said. "Then maybe we could go fishing. How about it?"

"Okay, Mom," Trevor said politely.

That didn't sound like my brother, either. He loves to go fishing—and he especially loves any trips that are just for him. (Not that the playground would be a thrill for me.) When breakfast was over, he quietly cleared his dishes and went to sit on the sofa until it was time to leave.

The minute Trevor and Mom were out the door, my father—who had been reading the paper at the kitchen table—called me in.

"Have a seat, honey," he invited me. I pulled out a chair, and Dad went on, "As you've probably guessed, Mom and I are a little worried about your brother."

I nodded. I was, too.

"Do you have any idea what's bothering him?" Dad asked.

Actually, I do, I wanted to say. *But it's not something I can tell you about.*

I was sure that Trevor was still worried about vampires—Vincent in particular.

Trevor had been there when Vincent told us he was a vampire. He had been right there because Vincent and Pittsy had—well, perhaps *kidnapped* is too strong a word. They had brought him to an old deserted lighthouse where Vincent had been hiding out, and had kept him hostage until I showed up. (That *is* kidnapping, as far as I'm concerned.)

Trevor had been right there when Vincent tried to bite my neck. He'd been there when a shaft of sunlight hit Vincent and destroyed him. He had watched as we dumped what was left of Vincent inside his coffin and slammed the coffin lid shut.

That's kind of a lot to see, for a kid who's not even in second grade yet. No wonder my brother wasn't feeling quite himself.

How could I explain that to my father? He'd never believe me! Trevor and I had never told Mom and Dad about Vincent's true identity. This certainly wouldn't be a good time to do it. I could just imagine how I'd sound: "Dad, remember that babysitter we had last year? Well, he turned out to be a vampire. . . ."

No, I couldn't do it. In any case, telling Dad

the truth wouldn't help Trevor. It wasn't as if there was anything Dad could do.

Forget the truth, I decided.

"I—I don't really know what's bothering Trev," I said, crossing my fingers mentally. "Maybe he's worried about going back to school or something."

Dad frowned. "Maybe. Anyway, Meggie, Mom and I would be grateful if you could make a special effort to spend more time with Trevor during the next couple of weeks. You know—include him in your plans a little more, take him to the beach once in a while. Stuff like that. As long as he's going through this stage, I think we should all do what we can to make him feel more secure.

"I know that's asking a lot," Dad added. "You're so much older than Trevor that he'll probably cramp your style. But—"

I giggled. "I don't *have* a style, Dad. I don't even have much to do, with Jack being at sailing camp and Pit—Kelly starting her babysitting job. Sure, I'll spend more time with Trevor. He's not bad, for a little brother."

"That's great. Thanks, Meg." I could see that Dad was relieved. "Oh—you can start tonight, by the way. Mom and I are going out to the Kollers' for dinner. You're Trevor's favorite babysitter, you know."

At least I'm not a vampire, I thought.

* * *

Trevor seemed to have cheered up a lot by the time Mom and Dad went out for the evening. He hardly flinched when they said they'd be out until quite late. He was even happier when I said I'd play Monopoly with him. I think Monopoly is the most boring game in the history of the universe, but for some reason my brother likes it. And by the time I was about to pass out with boredom, Trevor had started yawning himself.

"I think I'll go up to bed," he said. "Can I have my door open?"

"Absolutely," I told him.

"And will you make noise so I'll know where you are? You know, kind of walk loudly and clear your throat every once in a while?"

"No problem."

"And will you tell me when you come upstairs to go to bed, if I'm still awake?"

"For sure."

"And if I get scared, can I come sleep in your room?"

"Yup."

"And if I get hungry in the middle of the night if I'm sleeping in your room, will you go downstairs and get me some cookies?"

"No way."

Trevor wasn't surprised. "I didn't think so," he said. "But everything else is okay?"

"Everything else is okay."

Once my brother was in bed, I did the dishes as loudly as I could, clanging pots together and making sure to drop a few pieces of silverware. Then I stomped around the living room, straightening things up and talking out loud to the cat. All that noise must have calmed Trev right down because when I went up to check on him, he was sound asleep.

"I'm getting ready for bed now, Trev," I whispered, patting his shoulder gently. "Good night."

He mumbled something I couldn't understand and pushed his face into his pillow.

Ever since Vincent became a—well, part of my life, I've stopped reading horror stories at night. Now I always pick the blandest, dullest, sweetest stuff I can find. Which is why I chose an old *Brownie Girl Scout Handbook* the night I was babysitting for Trevor. At just about the point where I read that Swiss Brownies are called "Little Bees" and their troops are called "hives," the book slid out of my hands and thunked to the floor. I was too drowsy to pick it up, but I managed to turn off my bedside lamp before I fell asleep myself.

It couldn't have been midnight when I woke

up again. This time it was my turn to be waked up by a nightmare: I dreamed that I had been locked inside a freezer. When I woke up, I realized that I hadn't exactly been dreaming. My room *was* as cold as a freezer.

It does get awfully cold on Moose Island at night—down to the forties, sometimes. Everyone in my family sleeps with lots of blankets. But the cold that woke me was not the ordinary chill of a Maine island at night. It was a stabbing, deadly, bone-clenching cold. I could see my breath in front of my face.

I must have kicked off the covers, I thought as I fumbled to reach for them. But my blankets were drawn up under my chin. They just weren't working. I might as well have been covered with a piece of tissue paper.

"M-Meg?" called my brother in a thin, quavery voice. "I n-n-need you!"

"I'm coming," I called back as reassuringly as I could.

Really, I could hardly bear to get out of bed. The floor felt like frozen iron, and I was shaking so hard I could barely walk. But I managed to switch on my bedside lamp and make it into Trevor's room.

Trevor had gathered himself into a little ball under his covers. I dragged the blankets off the other bed in his room and piled them on top of him.

"Sh-shove over," I ordered. "I'm getting in with you. We'll be warmer that way."

Only a little warmer, though. The two of us took a long time to thaw out enough to talk.

"What do you think's the matter, Meg?" Trevor finally whispered. "Did winter come all of a sudden?"

"No, no. This is just a cold snap," I told him. "I wish I knew how to turn on the furnace. But I guess we'll have to wait until Mom and Dad come—"

Then we heard the scratching.

It was a thin, dry, delicate rasping from one corner of the ceiling. As if someone, or something, was stealing across the attic floor. . . .

"What's that?" asked Trevor tensely.

"Just a mouse in the wall," I said mock-cheerfully. "He must have come inside to get out of the cold."

The scratching came again, from a different corner. Then again, from directly over our heads.

"More than one mouse, I guess," said Trevor bravely.

"Maybe it's a whole family," I answered.

Then we heard a rustling, as though something

small and soft was being dragged across the floor. This sound, too, gradually increased until the whole ceiling above us was alive with rustling and stirring and gently scratching sounds.

"That's not mice!" my brother whispered. "It's ghosts! Meg, the house is haunted!"

I tried to laugh, but I wasn't too successful. "Houses don't *really* get haunted, silly," I said.

"Then why is it so cold in here?"

It was, indeed, much colder than before. The pillow felt like a block of ice, and it hurt to breathe. I wanted nothing so much as to pull my head under the covers—to shut out the noise and cold as best I could. But I had to be responsible.

I had to find out what was up in the attic—and try to get rid of it, if I possibly could.

Yeah, right, I found myself thinking. *Get rid of a million mice.*

What was I going to do—politely ask them to leave? Sic Pooch on them? (I could just see trying *that.* He'd lie there purring while they nibbled off his fur to make nests.)

And what if it *wasn't* mice upstairs? I didn't mention to Trevor that ghosts weren't what I was worried about. What if it was a crazed killer who had entered the house through the attic window?

Maybe that rustling sound was him dragging ropes or a net—something he'd brought with him to get rid of our bodies!

I could call the police, I thought. But I'd look awfully feeble if they showed up and found nothing but a couple of mice. . . .

Naturally I didn't voice these thoughts to my brother. I just told him I was going up to the attic to check on things.

"It'll only take a minute," I said. "You stay under the covers and wait for me."

I bet this is the kind of thing parents really hate about being grown up. Whenever someone hears a spooky noise, they're the ones who have to check it out—even though they probably feel like hiding, too.

And whenever a babysitter hears a spooky noise, she's the one who has to check it out—even though she *definitely* feels like hiding under the covers just as much as her brother does.

So, hunched and trembling with cold, I tiptoed across the frozen floor and out into the hall.

The house seemed to be listening as I inched up the attic stairs.

Listening as I quietly pulled open the door at the top of the stairs.

Listening as I took my first cautious step into the attic and fumbled for the light switch.

Listening for the shriek that tore out of my throat as I saw the hundreds—no, thousands—of bats that had been waiting for me.

CHAPTER FIVE

In a fiendish cloud the bats hurled themselves at me. I could feel their feathery softness and spiked wings brush against my face. I closed my eyes and doubled up, but there was no avoiding them. They were crawling all over me, their toes scrabbling for a foothold and their teeth searching for a tender spot to bite. . . .

"Meg! What's the matter?" My brother was anxiously calling from the bottom of the attic stairs. "Are you all right?"

With a *whoosh* the bats swirled up into the air and flew down the stairs toward him.

Trevor screamed and threw himself facedown on the ground. But the bats didn't want him. They flew back upstairs, whirled around me for an instant—and then disappeared through the open window at the end of the attic.

Trevor ran up the stairs to watch them.

I drew a long, shaky breath. "I—I guess that's what we were hearing downstairs," I said idiotically.

"What did they *want*?" Trevor asked in awe.

"Oh, nothing," I said lightly. "Probably just to come inside where it's warmer. Speaking of that, isn't it warming up in here again?" The attic felt like its regular chilly self now—not like the deep freeze it had seemed earlier.

Acting calmer than I felt, I strode over to the open window and shut it firmly. "Let's go back to bed," I said. "They won't be back to bother us."

I slept in Trevor's room just the same.

I had calmed Trevor down as best I could, but the next morning I could see that the memory of the bats was still frightening him. (It was frightening me, too, of course. Terrifying me, in fact. I had no idea what to make of it all.) None of the activities I suggested interested my brother. The beach would be too rough, he thought. "A riptide might drag us under," he said solemnly. He also thought a walk in the woods would be too dangerous. "We might fall into a pit." He even vetoed the idea of fishing off the dock behind our house. "A fishhook might catch in our eye."

"Maybe we should just take a nap," I finally suggested, feeling a little exasperated. In the mood Trevor was in, he'd probably worry that the bed would cave in and crush him. "Come on, Trev," I said. "We can just *sit* on the beach. We don't have to swim if you don't want to."

"Okay. I guess." Trevor sighed. "I wish this was the olden days, though," he said. "When people wore those long bathing suits that covered their legs. I bet the mosquitoes on the beach could give you malaria."

"Gee, Trev, I don't see any of your friends around," I said disappointedly when we got to the public beach. I had hoped that playing with someone his own age would take Trevor's mind off his troubles, but it would be up to me to distract him.

"Let's make a sand castle," I suggested. "We can put lots of—"

"Meg! Trevor! Hi!"

It was Pittsy, but I couldn't see her anywhere.

"Over here!" she shouted again, and this time I saw her. She and Vaughn Grimm were sitting under a beach umbrella, in the shade of a huge rock. Vaughn—who, I was startled to see, looked like a tiny gravedigger in a black turtleneck, black sweatpants, and tiny black cloth shoes—was carefully ladling sand into his diaper bag. (I hoped there wasn't any food in it.) Pittsy was lolling back against the rock and filing her nails, looking even more bored than usual.

"At last, someone who speaks English," she greeted me. "Do you have any gum?"

"Nope. Sorry," I told her. Trevor plopped down on the sand and began digging with the baby, who looked thrilled to have some attention. "What are you doing here in the shade?" I asked. "Why aren't you out in the sun getting skin cancer?"

"Oh, come on. There's no such thing as skin cancer. I bet those doctors just say that so they can have all the beaches to themselves. But I have to be responsible for the baby," Pittsy said with a grimace. "Vaughnie's very sensitive to the sun. And that reminds me—"

She pulled a sandy tube of sunscreen out of the beach bag and squeezed a huge glob of it into her palm. "Come here a second, Vaughn," she commanded. When he didn't obey—what did Pittsy think he was, a *dog*?—she picked him up with her free hand and began spreading sunscreen like frosting over his face.

"Hey! Not so much!" I said. Vaughn was whimpering and struggling in Pittsy's arms. "You'll get it in his eyes!"

"Didn't you hear what I said? He's, like, totally allergic to the sun."

"But you're sitting in the shade!"

"Doesn't matter," said Pittsy. "The Grimms told me I have to put sunscreen on him once an hour, sun or shade.

"You'll understand when you're old enough to babysit," she added maddeningly. "There, Vaughn. You can play again." She yanked his black turtleneck more securely over his chubby stomach. "Keep this shirt tucked in, and I won't have to put sunscreen on your tummy."

"What's all the black for?" I asked. "Are you taking him to a funeral?"

"Now, Meg," said Pittsy, in exactly Mrs. Grimm's voice. "You *know* babies need to make their own clothing selections to teach them that their choices *matter*. This is what he picked," she added in her regular voice. "All he wants is black stuff now. Don't ask me. I just go along with it. At least he picked regular clothes today. Yesterday all he wanted to wear was a black *scarf*. I had to tie it around his waist like a sash."

"He's really cute, though," said Trevor admiringly. He was tickling Vaughn now, and the baby was squealing with laughter.

"Yeah, I guess," Pittsy agreed. "I mean, he's not the most interesting person to *talk* to, but—"

Strangely, Vaughn picked that exact moment to talk—even though none of us knew what he was saying. A sea gull flew over our heads, and the baby glanced up with interest when the bird's shadow passed over his face.

"Bah! Bah!" he shouted happily, kicking his plump legs up and down in the sand. "Bah! Bah! Bah!"

"Bird? Is that what you said?" asked Pittsy. "Yes, that's a bird."

"AAAAAAAAAAAAAAAAGH!" was the baby's surprising answer. He shrieked it at full volume, hurling himself facedown in the sand and slamming his fists up and down. Then, still shrieking, he rolled over onto his back and began to flail at the air. In those few seconds his face had turned a dark, mottled purple.

"What is the *matter* with you, Vaughn?" Pittsy could hardly be heard above the baby's yowls. "All I said was bir—"

"AAAAAAAAAAAAAAAAGH!" the baby shrieked again. "Nuh-nuh-nuh-nuh-nuh-nuh-NUH!" It wasn't hard to guess that he meant "no."

"Maybe Trevor and I should go," I said. "He's getting awfully excited."

Besides, the afternoon had waned, and it was starting to cool off. I suddenly wanted to go home and sit in front of a cozy fire with Pooch.

"I'll come with you," Pittsy decided. "I think

the baby's tired. Maybe he'll take a nap in his stroller on the way home."

I had to admit she sounded as though she'd learned a lot about taking care of Vaughn. Maybe she did deserve this job.

Vaughn didn't fall asleep, although he did calm down after Pittsy finally succeeded in stuffing his writhing body into his stroller. He kept staring around him with bright black eyes, shouting random syllables and pointing at whatever caught his eye.

"Guh!" he yelled when we passed a Labrador retriever jogging along next to her owner. (Maybe "guh" meant "jog.") "Doy!" (I think that might have been "car.") "Dabadabadaba!" (I have no idea what a dabadabadaba is.)

We were passing an old, gnarled tree now. Just as we walked under it, a bat suddenly darted out of nowhere and looped crazily in front of us before skimming away again.

"BAH!" the baby screamed in huge excitement. "BAH! BAH! *BAH!*"

The finger he pointed at the bat was actually trembling.

"Bat?" I asked wonderingly. "Is that what you said before, too?"

Vaughn let out a delighted squeal and banged the sides of his stroller joyfully. "Bah!" he agreed.

You could see that he was relieved to have made his point at last.

"That's amazing!" I said, turning to Pittsy. "Where did he learn about bats?"

"I don't know."

Pittsy's voice was utterly flat.

"I have no idea," she said. "I didn't teach it to him, if that's what you're implying."

"I wasn't implying anything!" I protested. "I think it's cool that he can say—"

"That probably wasn't what he was saying, anyway," Pittsy cut in. "He was just babbling. Of course he doesn't know what a bat is! He's a *baby*!"

She gave me a guarded glance, as if she was trying to see how much of this I was buying.

"I-I've got to get him home," she said. "I think it's going to rain. See you around!"

She slung the baby's diaper bag over her shoulder and pushed the stroller away so quickly that I could see the baby jiggle whenever they went over a bump.

Trevor and I turned and stared at each other. The sky was a peaceful late-afternoon blue with a few pinkish clouds on the horizon to prepare us for the sunset.

"It's not going to rain, is it?" asked Trevor.

"I don't think so," I answered in a dazed voice.

"Then why did Pittsy say that?"

I shook my head. "I have absolutely no idea," I said. "Something's going on, but I don't know what."

CHAPTER SIX

For the next couple of days I couldn't get Pittsy out of my head. Had she been worried about something? Was that why she'd rushed away like that? Was she *hiding* something? Why did it matter whether Vaughn could say *bat* or not?

Since there was no way I could answer any of these questions, I gradually stopped thinking about them. Then one afternoon, a week or so later, I got a frantic phone call from Pittsy herself.

"You've got to help me!" she wailed. "My mother says I have to go to the dentist! It's so *stupid* because we *have* a dentist at home, and I don't see why I have to see one *here,* too, but she says it's *time*! Isn't that *revolting*?"

I paused and finally said, "I guess so, but I don't see how I can help. Do you want me to come along or something?"

"No, it's not that." Pittsy took a deep breath. "The thing is, I'm supposed to take care of

Vaughn this afternoon. I *told* my mother over and over that she should make my appointment for sometime when I *wouldn't* have anything else to do, but she's so, like, *inconsiderate* that she just went ahead and scheduled me for this afternoon! She says she told me about this two weeks ago, but she didn't because I would have *remembered,* right? I've got a very alert mind."

"So how can I help?" I asked patiently. "Do you want me to babysit for Vaughn?"

"Oh, *would* you?" Pittsy sounded as though the idea had just occurred to her. "I'm sure that would be okay with the Grimms. You could keep the pay, too," she added generously. "I mean, you wouldn't have to share it with me or anything."

I hadn't been planning to.

"It's at one o'clock this afternoon," Pittsy went on. "One till five."

"Do you think it'll be okay if I bring my brother?" I asked. I was still doing my best to keep Trevor occupied.

"Sure," Pittsy said. "The baby will like having another kid there. One o'clock. Don't be late, okay?"

There may be someone on this planet who's ruder than Pittsy, but I doubt it.

* * *

"It's a scary-looking house, Meg," Trevor whispered as we walked up the front path at one that afternoon. "And I hate that statue guy over there. Doesn't he look as though he's staring at us?"

"That's the way he's *made* to look," I said reassuringly—even though I myself had been watching the statue rather uneasily. "And the house is really all right. They're just fixing it—"

The front door opened just then, so I didn't get to finish. A harried-looking Mrs. Grimm peered out at us. When I heard the screams coming from behind her, I could see why she was harried. The baby sounded as if someone were torturing him.

"Vaughnie's a little bit fussy today," Mrs. Grimm told us unnecessarily as she led us into the house. "Teething, I think. He's up in his crib now. I thought maybe he'd go down for a nap"—she sighed—"but I'm starting to doubt it. You'll probably have to get him up and play with him.

"Just let him do whatever he wants," she added. "It will cheer him up. He can have whatever he wants to eat—and you help yourselves, too. 'Sesame Street' is on at three, and he always likes watching that. Oh! And if you take him outside, please be *sure* to put lots of sunscreen on him—it's in the basket on his changing table. He's terribly sensitive to the sun. Well, see you later!"

She looked as if she was glad to escape from that house of torment.

When the front door was closed, Trevor and I looked at each other and shrugged. "I guess we might as well go up and get Vaughn," I said. "Maybe he'll cheer up when he sees us."

To my surprise, he did. He had been thrashing around in his crib when we opened the door and tiptoed in, but the second he saw us he pulled himself upright and grinned wetly at us. "Bah!" he shouted, jouncing up and down. "Bah!"

"Bat?" I asked wonderingly. "Do you remember that time on the beach last week?" It seemed hard to believe.

"BAH!" the baby shouted more insistently. And he pointed into the corner behind us.

Trevor and I both turned to look, but all we saw was a basket of stuffed animals. "There's no bat here," I said. "See, it's just your toys. Look—"

Suddenly I stopped. Poking out from under a fluffy toy poodle was a black bat's wing. "Is this what you mean?" I asked.

I reached gingerly into the basket and pulled out the wing with my fingertips. It was attached to a large, black, extremely realistic rubber bat.

Vaughn screamed with excitement when he saw it. For a second I thought he was going to hurl himself out of his crib.

"Bah! Bah! Bah!" he shrieked, reaching desperately over the top of his crib. "Bah! Bah! Bah! BAH!"

"Okay! Okay!" I said, rushing over. "Here it is!"

Vaughn grabbed the bat and cuddled it against his cheek. "Bah," he crooned adoringly. He could have been in a TV commercial, if the object he was holding hadn't been a bat.

And he'd have to be dressed a little differently. Once again, Vaughn was entirely swaddled in black. A black polo shirt, black jeans, miniature black high-tops—it was all very cool, but not very babylike.

"Where do they buy this stuff?" I wondered aloud as I reached in and lifted the crooning baby out of his crib. "Not on Moose Island, that's for sure." The one baby store on the island was as pastel as an Easter egg.

"Black makes him look so pale, too," Trevor pointed out. "Don't most babies have—you know—rosy cheeks and stuff? Vaughn looks like a ghost!"

As I glanced more closely at the baby, I realized that my brother was right. Vaughn's skin was more than pale. It was a chalky, dull-looking gray. If he hadn't been acting so healthy, I would have worried that he was coming down with something.

"The Grimms do put an awful lot of sunscreen on him," I pointed out uneasily. "Oh, well. I'm sure they'd have let us know if anything was the matter. Let's take him downstairs and give him a snack."

Vaughn was very interested when I opened the refrigerator door for him. He toddled forward and stared inside. Finally he patted a leftover piece of tomato-covered meat loaf wrapped in plastic. "Da," he said.

"Meat loaf? You're sure?" I asked. "Well, okay." I plopped Vaughn in his high chair and set the meat loaf on the tray in front of him. Immediately he starting crumbling it up and dropping bloody-looking bits onto the floor. (That *is* the way most babies eat, isn't it?)

"I'm hungry, too," said Trevor hopefully. "She said we could have something to eat, didn't she?"

"Yup," I told him. "Let's see what's in here." I reached in and took out some cold fried chicken, a batch of lasagna, and half an apple pie. "Pretty good leftovers," I commented. "Do you want any of this?"

"I guess some pie, please," said my brother.

I cut him a slice and then reached for the lasagna. I hadn't had time for lunch before we left, and the lasagna looked perfect. "I'll just microwave this," I said, pulling the plastic wrap off the plate.

"Whew!" I added as the fumes from the lasagna began curling up toward me. "There's a lot of garlic in this! Maybe I'll have something else—"

Suddenly the baby let out a shrill scream and doubled up in his high chair as if something were hurting him. "Nuh-nuh-nuh!" he wailed helplessly.

"What's the matter, Vaughn?" I asked in a panic. "Are you sick? Maybe a pin is sticking you!" I lifted him out of his high chair to check.

"He doesn't wear cloth diapers, does he?" asked Trevor. "Doesn't he wear the kind with tape?"

"Oh, yeah. You're right." The baby was still screaming and writhing in my arms. I sat down with him, but his screaming only got worse.

"He looks as though he's trying to get away from something," Trevor observed. It was true. The baby kept trying to fling himself away from the kitchen table.

"Could you please hold him a sec so I can put the lasagna away?" I asked my brother. "I'll have to have lunch later." I passed the writhing, wailing baby to Trevor and covered the lasagna again.

Instantly Vaughn's cries stopped. "Dah-doy," he said calmly.

"I didn't know lasagna made babies cry," Trevor said, sounding too loud in the sudden quiet.

"Maybe it's the smell of the garlic," I said. "Let me just check—"

I pulled off one corner of the plastic wrap.

Vaughn's face screwed up piteously, and he took a deep breath as if he were about to start screaming again. Quickly I re-covered the dish—again he cheered up.

This was very strange. Against my will I remembered someone else who hadn't liked the smell of garlic.

Vincent Graver, our vampire babysitter. Trevor and I had once offered him some pizza with garlic, and he had practically taken our heads off. In fact, I remembered, he hadn't even been able to stay in the same room when a commercial for garlic bread was on TV.

I gave myself a mental shake. Vaughn had nothing in common with Vincent except they both had weird first names. I was letting my imagination get the better of me again, and that wasn't good for any of us.

"Let's take the baby outside," I suggested. "We could all use some fresh air."

Actually, the air was a little *more* fresh than I would have liked. It was kind of cold and gray outside. (I put sunscreen on Vaughn all the same, of course.) But the baby was delighted to get outside. He headed right for the fountain and started paddling his hands in the water.

"Oh, Vaughn, I wish you wouldn't do that," I said weakly. "You'll get awfully wet."

I have to admit that I wasn't as worried about the baby's getting wet as I was about standing near the statue. I couldn't stand the sight of that evil stone face. But when I tried to pick up the baby and carry him somewhere else, he screamed so loudly that I gave up.

"Mrs. Grimm said to let him do whatever he wants," I reminded myself out loud. "I guess this won't hurt him."

Trevor wasn't listening. He was staring up at the stone statue with a look of fear in his eyes.

"M-Meg," he began and had to clear his throat to get the words out. "Meg, doesn't this statue remind you of someone?"

I stared reluctantly up at the ugly figure looming over us. It stared menacingly down at me, and I realized that Trevor was right. There *was* something strangely familiar about the statue, but I wasn't sure why or what.

"I-I don't think so," I said. "I sure hope we don't know anyone who looks like that."

I glanced down at the baby, who was laughing gaily and splashing in the fountain. "Vaughn likes him, anyway," I said. "He certainly has—well, unusual tastes."

Trevor sighed. "This is an awfully gloomy house, though," he said. "I'm kind of scared."

"Oh, you don't need to be." I tried to sound cheerful. "The house just looks gloomy because it's so gray out. If there were a little sunshine, we'd—"

As if a string somewhere in heaven had been pulled, the clouds slid back and a shaft of sunlight streamed down toward us. For the moment it brightened everything. The water in the fountain turned a sparkling blue. The dew on the damp grass gleamed like crystal. A bird in the hedge started to chirp cheerfully.

And Vaughn had another temper tantrum.

Not *temper,* exactly. Anyone could see that the sun was making him terribly uncomfortable. I've told you about his screaming already, but let me just say that he was screaming worse than ever now. He rubbed his eyes in pain and buried his head in my shoulder. He didn't calm down until the clouds covered the sun and everything was gray again.

A baby who didn't like the sun . . .

Once again my mind turned unwillingly toward Vincent. This time I could see that Trevor's thoughts were running along the same lines.

"Meg," he said slowly, not meeting my eyes, "didn't the sun kind of—bother Vincent?"

Yes, the sun had bothered Vincent. If you can call turning someone into a shriveled husk "bothering" him.

"And Vincent was Pittsy's friend, right?"

I nodded.

"And you were worried that maybe Vincent had turned Pittsy into a"—Trevor gulped—"into a vampire."

"But I'm sure he didn't," I said hastily. I didn't want Trev worrying like this. "I mean, look at her! She doesn't act like a—"

My brother interrupted me. "No, she doesn't," he agreed. "But Vaughn does."

I started to answer, but I couldn't think of anything to say. If Trevor had noticed the same things I had, we were probably right.

"He—he likes bats," Trevor faltered. "He hates the sun. He hates garlic. He wears all black. He likes food that's all dripping with tomato sauce, like blood. He's kind of gray, the way Vincent was. Are his teeth pointed?"

Just then the baby gave us a sweet, innocent smile.

The smile answered Trevor's question.

Vaughn didn't have many teeth. In fact, he had only four. They were set outside the space where his front upper and lower teeth would grow—and they were most definitely pointed.

"Meg, it's happening again!" My brother's voice was quavering. "Vincent *must* have turned Pittsy into a vampire. Because now she's turning the baby into a vampire!"

CHAPTER SEVEN

"I-I don't quite know what to tell you, Trevor," I said slowly. "I mean, I'm your big sister. I don't want you to be scared of anything.

"On the other hand, I think you're right. The baby *is* acting like a vampire. And who could be causing that but Pittsy?"

In silence my brother and I stared down at little Vaughn, who was smiling up at us while he sloshed the fountain water around. His pointed teeth were *very* strange now that I really looked at them. I wondered why I hadn't noticed them before.

I cleared my throat. "Well," I said briskly, "we're still his babysitters no matter what, and I'm afraid he'll get too wet and cold if we stay out here any longer." I checked my watch. "His favorite show is almost on. Let's bring him back inside for it."

We settled ourselves down on the floor in the

den, gave Vaughn a few toys to bash around while he watched, and turned on PBS.

It had been awhile since I'd seen "Sesame Street." I had forgotten that one of the characters on the show was a puppet named Count von Count. The Count (who, you may not be surprised to hear, loves to count things) wears a long black cape, lives in a bat-filled castle, and generally acts like a cute version of—you guessed it—Dracula.

As I say, it had been so long since I'd seen the show that I had forgotten about the Count—but the baby hadn't.

When the Count came on, Vaughn let out a delighted squeal. He rushed up to the screen and planted a big wet kiss on it. "Bah! Bah!" he said excitedly.

"More evidence," said Trevor gloomily.

When the Count's scene ended, Vaughn burst into tears. In fact, he cried so long and so hard that I finally decided to try putting him down for a nap again. This time he cuddled down into his crib and fell asleep instantly.

I tiptoed downstairs and found my brother in the den. "Meg, can we go home now?" he asked timidly. "This house is really scaring me."

"Of course we can't, silly," I said as heartily as I could. "We can't leave Vaughn alone in the house!"

Trevor's chin quivered. "*I* don't want to be alone in the house with *him*!"

"Now, wait a minute, Trev." I sat down next to my brother and put a hand on his shoulder. "We don't know for sure that he's turning into a vampire. And even if he is, he's still a baby. A vampire baby's not nearly so bad as a grown-up vampire." *I hope not, anyway. . . .*

I jumped to my feet so my thoughts wouldn't start to wander. "You know what I think? I think we should search the house for clues."

"What kind of clues?" asked Trevor.

"Oh, vampire-type clues. Something that'll tell us whether we're on the right track or not." I didn't expect to find much of anything. I just wanted to give Trevor something to do besides brood. "Come on," I urged him. "It will be fun to snoop around this house anyway."

It wasn't exactly fun, but we did turn up a few weird surprises. The little closet under the back stairs held a two-foot-tall stone owl with a stone mouse clutched in its talons. The old mirror on the landing had a faded leather glove tucked behind it. There was a bouquet of dead flowers in one of the bathrooms. And under the refrigerator was a little plastic Barbie shoe. I bet that nine out of ten houses in the United States have a Barbie something under the refrigerator. Barbie is certainly careless with her stuff.

Either Mrs. Grimm was fond of unusual decorative touches, or she just hadn't gotten around to clearing out the junk the previous owners had left. In any case, none of this stuff was a *clue.*

"So much for our detective work," I said to Trevor. "Unless we want to go through their bureaus—and I don't—I guess we won't turn up much. I think I hear Vaughn waking up, anyway. Let's go get him."

It was while I was changing the baby that I found the only clue we were to discover that day. There was a stack of diapers on one side of the changing table, and when I picked one up, I noticed something glinting at the bottom of the pile. I lifted the diapers away to see . . .

"What is this thing?" I asked Trevor, mystified. "What's it doing in the baby's room?"

It was an oval about three inches in diameter, made out of what appeared to be carved dark gray bone. At first I thought it was a door knocker, but it wasn't thick enough for that. Besides, what door knocker had ever had a red stone set in its center? A smooth oval stone so deep in color that it was almost black. . . .

Trevor's face was pale. "It's Vincent's ring!" he gasped. "It's that ring you found when we first got here this summer!"

Almost two months ago, on the day we'd arrived at our summer house, I had found an old ring that turned out to be Vincent's. Not realizing whose it was, I had worn it for a few weeks—and not realizing that the ring made the wearer psychic, I hadn't paid any attention to the strange warnings it sent me about Vincent and his return to the island.

It was true that this ring was almost exactly like that other one. "But this can't be that same ring," I said blankly. "A bat flew off with that ring! Besides, that ring was made of metal. And it was—well—*ring-size*. This one is much too big for anyone's finger."

"Maybe it's a bracelet," Trevor suggested. "Do vampires wear bracelets? But I guess it's too big for that, unless they had really, really fat—"

Just then Vaughn caught sight of the strange ring. He let out an eerie cackle. With startling monkeylike speed, he reared up, grabbed it out of my hand, and stuffed it into his mouth. A second later he was lolling back on his changing table, contentedly gumming the dark red stone.

"Trevor, it's a *teething* ring," I whispered. "A vampire's teething ring."

I was sure I was right on both counts. Vaughn was obviously so used to teething on this ring that that *had* to be what it was for. And, except for its size, the teething ring was identical to the ring I had found earlier that summer.

What, I wondered, did gnawing on a vampire's teething ring do to a baby's teeth? Did it make them grow in *pointed*?

If so, it was already working. . . .

My mind was working, too. Earlier this summer Pittsy had tried and tried to make me give her that first ring. (Vincent had asked her to get it for him, and she thought he wanted to give it to her as an engagement ring. As you've probably guessed by now, she's not too bright.) In fact, her *not* getting the ring was what had led her to kidnap Trevor and bring him to Vincent. But that's another story.

Pittsy had to be the link to *this* ring, the teething ring. Because who else in the Grimm household could possibly have come by such a thing? Where would they have found it?

It can't be a coincidence, I said to myself. Two rings, identical in everything but size, could hardly turn up in the same summer without there being some connection. Pittsy must be—

A voice broke into my thoughts at that point. "Yoo-hoo! Hi, guys!"

Mrs. Grimm was home.

"Good." Trevor sounded relieved. "Let's get out of here."

I picked Vaughn up—he was still firmly attached to the teething ring—and we headed downstairs with him.

"Hello there! How'd everything go?" Mrs. Grimm scooped up the baby and gave him a big kiss. "Was Vaughnie a good boy?"

"He was pretty happy most of the time," I said. "Once or twice he got a little upset, but he calmed down fast. He napped for about an hour."

"Wonderful. Oh, and you found his teething ring! That's fantastic! Where on earth was it?" asked Mrs. Grimm.

"On his changing table, under a pile of diapers," I said.

Mrs. Grimm shook her head regretfully. "Gee, I wish I'd known that earlier. Vaughnie loves that teething ring. He doesn't sleep half as well at night without it."

"It's a very, um, unusual teething ring," I said carefully. "Where did you get it?"

"That's a funny thing, Meg—I'm not sure," said Mrs. Grimm. "I found it in the front hall about two weeks ago. There was no card with it, and I never found out who'd sent it."

Pittsy, I was sure. She'd probably been trying to cover her tracks.

"But the baby certainly adores it," Mrs. Grimm went on. "I can't say it's making his teeth come in any faster, but he's trying." She sighed. "I'll be glad when his front teeth come in. It's so jarring to see him with just his canines."

"Canines?" Trevor and I echoed together.

"Yes. The teeth on the outside of the front four teeth are called canines. They're pointed, like dogs' teeth—that's how they got their name. Vaughn's pediatrician says it's very rare to have a baby's canines come in first. In fact, he said he'd never seen it happen before, but it's perfectly normal. Isn't it, Vaughnie?" she cooed.

No, it's not, I wanted to tell her. *It's not normal at all.*

Mrs. Grimm paid me very well for taking care of Vaughn. She even gave Trevor a tip, which made him feel very grown up. "I can see that the baby likes you both," she said. "I hope you'll be free to substitute any time Kelly can't make it."

"Well, we won't," Trevor whispered as we set off on the hedged front path. "I'm never going back in that vampire house again."

I didn't answer. I was sure *I* would be going back to the Grimms' house before too long. I couldn't let Pittsy carry out her terrible plan without trying to stop her.

I wasn't going to stand by and watch an innocent child become a vampire.

Or was I?

I tried not to look at the fountain as Trevor and I scurried past, but for one fleeting second it was impossible to avoid seeing the statue's face.

I tried to stifle a gasp, but Trevor heard me. "What's the matter?" he asked.

"Oh, nothing," I said weakly.

Trevor had had enough for one day. I didn't want to tell him that I'd suddenly realized why the stone statue seemed so familiar.

It was starting to look just like Vincent.

CHAPTER EIGHT

Pittsy burst into a flood of hysterical tears when I asked her, the next day, if she knew anything about the teething ring I'd found at the Grimms'.

"H-h-h-h-h-h-how can you be so, like, h-h-h-heartless?" she wailed, hurling herself facedown on her bed. (We were in her room.) "Are you t-t-t-t-trying to force me to remember how horribly that *monster* Vincent treated me?"

Tears were actually spurting out of her eyes. I was impressed, but I didn't let her put me off the track.

"I'm not trying to remind you of anything," I said. "I'm just asking whether you know how the teething ring got into the house. You didn't give it to the baby, did you?"

More tears came fountaining out. "Like I'd really give the *baby* something that would remind me of *Vincent*," Pittsy sobbed. "Like I'd really want to see something that looked like my *en-*

gagement ring stuck in a baby's *mouth* day in, day out, day in, day out, day in, day—"

"I get the point," I interrupted, a little meanly. "And you're trying to tell me that you've never even *seen* the teething ring when you've been over at the Grimms'?"

"Well, I—uh—" Pittsy stopped, biting her lip. "I may have kind of noticed it."

"What are you—"

"I hid it," Pittsy confessed in a rush.

I could only stare at her. "Why?"

Pittsy gave a throbbing sniff. "I didn't even want to *think* about anything that reminded me of Vincent."

"So you put it under a stack of *diapers*?"

"I thought that would be a good place," Pittsy said defensively. "I never change Vaughn if I can help it—I mean—"

I knew what she meant. Pittsy was the kind of babysitter who would put off changing a diaper for a year, if she could.

"Anyway, I would have had a total *nervous breakdown* if I had to keep seeing that stupid ring! Like what you're trying to give me now," she added brokenly. "Thanks a lot, Meg. All I can hope is, maybe someday your heart will be broken and someone younger than you will start rubbing it in the way you're doing to me."

She sniffed weakly, like a poor little invalid about to be wiped out by her great tragedy—but I thought she was checking out my reaction above her wadded-up tissue.

I gave up questioning Pittsy for the moment, though. Maybe she was faking all this emotion, but I didn't want to be around while she was wallowing in it. You'd have to be a lot better detective than I am to get the truth out of Pittsy without *killing* her first.

"How'd it go?" Trevor asked eagerly when I got home from talking to Pittsy. We were sitting at the kitchen table having some juice.

"Not great," I said and described the way she had acted.

When I'd finished, Trevor sighed. "I kind of thought she'd—you know—break down and confess that she was using the ring for evil purposes," he said. "And promise never to do it again."

"I guess Pittsy is tougher than that," I said. "And maybe she's smarter than I thought, too. Maybe she knew that blubbering on and on about Vincent would be the best way to get me to leave her alone."

"So what are we going to try next?" asked Trevor perkily.

I stared at him. "You mean what am *I* going to try next? You shouldn't get involved in this, Trev. It'll probably be pretty intense."

Trevor gulped down the rest of his juice and set his cup down with a snap. "No, I *want* to help you. I was thinking about it in the night."

His face was very serious. "I'm almost in second grade," he reminded me. "That's old enough to help with the chores."

"Yes, but getting rid of a vampire isn't your average chore!"

"I know, but I really want to help," Trevor said again. "It would make me even *more* worried to think that Pittsy might hurt Vaughn. Come on, Meg," he urged. "What if we were in the olden days and there was a blizzard and we needed wood and you were taking care of a sick cow or something? You'd *have* to let me chop that wood for you! Besides, you need a man to help you out now that Jack's at sailing camp."

"I'm going to ignore that last remark," I said with dignity. "I can take care of vampires perfectly well on my own, thank you. Other than that, I'd love to have you along." I leaned across the table and rumpled his hair. "Now that you're almost in second grade, I'm sure we can come up with a great plan for rescuing Vaughn."

* * *

"*This* was the best we could come up with?" I muttered under my breath as Trevor and I sneaked out the back door together. "Careful, Trev! Don't slam the door!"

We had to sneak out because it was after nine at night—not a time Mom and Dad would let us go for a walk, especially at the end of the summer, when it gets dark early. Most especially not on a stormy night, which this night definitely was.

Storm-tossed would be the word for it, I think. The wind was hurling the trees back and forth so hard that broken branches hit the ground like rain. There was no *real* rain, thank heaven, but the wind was whipping the clouds along so fast that we only caught stray flashes of the full moon. Whenever there was enough light, I could see the ocean rolling and boiling and smashing its way to shore.

Usually there wasn't enough light to see anything at all. As Trevor and I picked our way along the churning shoreline, we kept stumbling. "People don't set traps in the sand, do they?" Trevor gasped after one particularly bad fall.

I couldn't help laughing. "What for? To catch sand fleas?"

"I wish we were at the Grimms' already," was all Trevor answered.

I wasn't sure I wished that, but the Grimms' was where we were heading. Pittsy was baby-sitting for Vaughn. "It's going to be a late night," she had told me over the phone that morning. "The Grimms are going to a concert on the mainland. They'll be taking the twelve o'clock ferry back. So come on over and visit if you get bored. They said it would be okay for me to have a friend over."

Well, Trevor and I were both going over, but not as visitors. We were going as spies, on a mission. We were going to see if we could catch Pittsy in the act of turning the baby into a vampire. If we were going to take action against her, we needed proof first.

I was beginning to think we had made a mistake, though. How were we going to get into the Grimms' house? What if Pittsy caught us spying on her? What if the Grimms decided to take an earlier ferry home, and they caught us?

You're acting like Trevor, I told myself. *Stop worrying. Everything will be all—*

A huge, dark wave crashed onto shore just then, slapping the two of us to the ground and drenching us to the skin. I gritted my teeth and pulled Trevor to his feet for the millionth time.

I decided it would be enough if we got to the Grimms' without drowning. I'd worry about everything else later.

* * *

"There's the house," I said wearily as Trevor and I left the beach and headed up a path cut between the dunes. The Grimms' mansion loomed menacingly about a hundred feet ahead of us. I was relieved to see that lights were on in almost every downstairs room. If the Grimms were already home, they would probably have gone upstairs and turned out the downstairs lights. Pittsy, of course, would never care about saving electricity—especially someone else's.

"Follow me," I whispered to Trevor. We tiptoed toward the front of the house and started up the hedged pathway, glancing nervously from side to side. "Let's peek through the windows and see if we can spot her," I told him.

We leaned against the narrow, lead-paned windows, windows that looked like part of an ancient dungeon. The ones in the front of the house were almost hidden behind tall, spiky evergreens. I hoped we wouldn't make too much noise rustling around. . . .

"Meg! He's moving!"

Trevor's voice was hoarse with terror. He grabbed my sleeve and pointed a shaky hand at the statue in the fountain.

"I saw him turn around," he panted. "He's trying to get off the pedestal!"

I stared fixedly at the statue. In the flickering moonlight his face looked more evil than ever. But he was standing as still as any stone statue.

"He *did* move! I saw him out of the corner of my eye!" Trevor was almost crying. "He swished his cape around his shoulders and—"

"What cape? Trev, he's not wearing a cape!" I tried to laugh. "See? They're just some kind of wings."

Trevor rubbed his eyes. "I-I guess you're right," he said after a second. "But, Meg, it sure *looked* as if he had a cape."

"Must have been a low-flying sea gull," I said. "Just don't look at him."

What we're about to see will probably be even worse, I didn't add out aloud.

We squeezed ourselves in between the bushes and the front windows. "Ouch," Trevor blurted out in a loud, normal voice at one point—but there was no sign of Pittsy or the baby. The silent rooms with their sheet-draped furniture were empty of life.

"Let's go around to the side," I whispered.

A furious gust of wind chased a cloud across the moon and whipped the water in the fountain into a sea of tiny waves. Then, just as suddenly, the wind stopped—but only for an instant.

It was only long enough for me to hear footsteps walking lightly behind us.

I froze in my tracks. I hardly dared to turn around, but when I did, there was nothing there.

"I guess I was just imagining it," I said, relieved. "But—but, Meg," Trevor said, faltering, "can two people imagine the same thing at the same time?"

That stopped me. "You heard footsteps, too?"

My brother nodded. His eyes were enormous.

Now both of us slowly peered behind us. Still, all we could see was the windswept sky and the hedge on either side of the path. The statue stood motionless on its pedestal.

"Trev, I'm taking you home," I said with sudden decision. "This is too much for a kid your age."

"No! I want to stay!" he hissed. "Let's just try a few more windows."

If there were any more footsteps, we shut out their sound as we continued to search the windows. There was nothing to see in the cavernous dining room, nothing in the kitchen. (How could Mrs. Grimm stand to cook on that mammoth black stove? I wondered.) Nothing in the library, with its shelves and shelves of dusty leather books. Then in the den—

When we peeked through the den window, I relaxed at last. Why hadn't we realized Pittsy would be in there? The TV was there, after all!

And Pittsy was slumped in front of it, sound asleep.

"Good baby-sitting instincts," I muttered. "Well, Trevor, this time I guess we really *did* imagine—"

Then I saw the shadow creep into the den.

Both my brother and I took a hasty step backward, and Trevor grabbed my hand again. "Wh-what's that?" he asked in a quavering voice.

"Shhhh! I don't know," I whispered.

All I wanted to do was grab my brother and get out of there, but I couldn't leave Pittsy in danger! What was happening?

The shadow was hunching slowly toward her. It was low to the ground, and strangely lumpy looking. For a wild moment I wondered if it could be a raccoon.

Then I realized that it was the baby. Dressed in a long black nightshirt and carrying his toy rubber bat under one arm, he was half walking, half crawling through the dark toward Pittsy's chair. The nightshirt kept tripping him, but he kept going.

"It's just Vaughn!" I murmured in relief. "He must have climbed out of his crib and come down to find Pittsy. Poor little thing, I hope he wasn't scared or—"

Then Vaughn's face came out of the shadows.

This baby wasn't scared.

His mouth was open in a frightening snarl. His pointed teeth were gleaming white. His eyes were wide, and a fierce red light was burning out of them.

He resembled a wild animal more than a human baby.

Now he was crawling stealthily over to Pittsy's chair. He seemed to be getting more and more agile as he approached her—almost as if he were becoming less and less of a baby the closer he got. He was practically gliding by the time he reached Pittsy's feet.

Why didn't I call out, or bang on the window, or do *something* to wake Pittsy up? I asked myself that many times afterward. But at the time I just couldn't move.

So I watched in horrified fascination as the baby grabbed the arm of the chair and climbed swiftly up its side. I watched as he crawled nimbly across the top of the chair. I watched as he crept toward Pittsy and lifted his head.

Finally I watched as he prepared to sink his pointed teeth into her neck.

NEWS

CHAPTER NINE

Then I came to my senses and *did* bang on the window—as hard as I could.

"Wake up! *Wake up!*" I shrieked.

"Oh, stop him, Meg!" Trevor begged next to me. "Break the glass!"

But it turned out there was no need for that. When Vaughn heard us, he turned quickly to the window. For an instant the fierce light in his eyes glowed furiously—but in the next second the baby seemed to flick off a switch somewhere inside himself. His eyes became round and innocent again. He cocked his head cutely to one side. He gave me and Trevor a sweet, shy smile and a tiny wave of his chubby hand. Then he skittered down from the top of the chair, cuddled into Pittsy's lap, and went to sleep.

That woke Pittsy up. Startled, she glanced down at the sleeping baby.

I banged on the window again. "Let us in!" I called. "We have to talk to you!"

Pittsy stared at the window and then back down at Vaughn in groggy confusion. *What's he doing here?* I could tell she was wondering. She lifted him into her arms and stepped over to the window, rubbing her eyes with her free hand.

"Let us *in*!" I called again.

Pittsy frowned at me, but I couldn't hear what she said over the noise of the storm. She pointed to her watch and shook her head.

Of all the times for Pittsy to go *responsible* on me! I gestured frantically at the front door. "Please!" I mouthed.

Pittsy sighed and shrugged. Still holding the baby, she walked out of the den. Trevor and I untangled ourselves from the bushes and raced toward the front door. We were waiting there when Pittsy unlocked it.

"You can only stay for a couple of seconds," she said peevishly. "I've been trying to get Vaughn to fall asleep."

"No, you haven't," I contradicted her. "We were watching you in the den, and—"

"Okay! Okay!" said Pittsy. "So maybe I took a little nap! Who cares? It doesn't mean anything! The baby was sound asleep, and—"

"No, he wasn't," I contradicted her again. "He—"

"Anyway, why were you spying through the windows?" Pittsy cut in crossly. "Why couldn't you just come through the front door like normal people?"

"That's what we're trying to do now," I pointed out. "Come on, Kelly, let us in. No one's trying to pick on you."

"We're trying to *save* you," Trevor added importantly. (Now that Vaughn was asleep again, Trevor was feeling a little braver.) "You're in terrible, terrible danger."

"Yeah, really," Pittsy scoffed, but she let us in anyway.

"Let me just take the baby up to his crib," she said as we stood there in the hall. She shook her head in bewilderment. "I guess I must have brought him down and we both fell asleep or something."

"No way!" Trevor said. "He crawled out of his crib and tried to *attack*—"

"It'll keep, Trev," I said quickly. For some reason I felt uncomfortable talking about any of this stuff in front of Vaughn. He seemed to be sound asleep, but what if that was just an act? Considering the fierce-eyed demon he'd been just a few minutes before, nothing about this baby would have surprised me.

"Okay," said Pittsy a couple of minutes later as she rejoined us downstairs. "He's down for the count. Let's talk in the kitchen, okay? I'm starving. Babysitting really gives you an appetite."

All that sleeping must burn a lot of calories, I thought.

In the kitchen Pittsy yanked open a cupboard door, pulled out a bag of pretzels, and tossed them onto the table. "Juice, anyone?" she asked, crossing to the refrigerator. "Mrs. Grimm is such a moron about soda. She thinks it's junky. Like, she won't even buy it! Even diet soda! So whenever I'm here I have to ruin my figure with stupid *juice.*"

Pittsy plunked a bottle of cranberry juice onto the table disgustedly. "So," she said when we'd all helped ourselves, "what are you guys doing here, anyway?"

Trevor and I exchanged a glance. "You tell her, Meg," he said firmly. "You're older. She'll believe you more."

So—hoping that she would believe me even a little—I told Pittsy everything.

About how we'd found the teething ring and gotten worried. About coming to the Grimms' house to make sure everything was all right. About seeing the baby crawling into the room. About how he had tried to bite her in the neck.

"So that's why we were watching you," I finished apologetically. "We started out thinking *you* were the vampire. At least now we know you're not. That's a plus, isn't it?"

Pittsy didn't answer. She just frowned down into the bottom of her juice glass.

"Isn't it?" I repeated.

Still Pittsy was silent. Then she stood up and pushed in her chair with a snap.

"I'm going home," she announced. "I'm calling my dad to come get me right now. I'm not staying in this house with you two for one minute longer."

Trevor and I exchanged another glance. "What do you mean?" Trevor asked in a tiny voice.

"I *mean,* you came all this way just to remind me of my tragedy with Vincent *again*! Why do you, like, keep rubbing my nose in it? It's not fair! Why can't *you* have some kind of romance that *I* can make fun of?"

I could tell Pittsy was really furious. Her face was all blotchy red, and she was clenching her fists without even thinking about her manicure.

"And picking on a poor little baby, too!" she went on. "As if little Vaughn would really be a *vampire.* He loves me! He thinks I'm better than his mother! He can't wait for me to come—"

"Look in the mirror," I interrupted quietly.

"Huh?" Pittsy broke off and glared at me.

I pointed at the little mirror hanging next to the sink. "Look at your neck. There are tooth marks in it."

Two tiny spots, a little lighter than Pittsy's skin, made a delicate design on her throat.

"I-I can't believe it," Pittsy whispered, staring at her reflection. "You mean that Vaughnie—that a little *baby* could—" She broke off, still staring at herself. "Boy," she added, almost with pride. "Vampires sure are, like, attracted to me! My chemistry must really fascinate them. It's a curse, I guess."

Abruptly she changed the subject. "Now, let's see. Where did I leave my bag?"

"What bag?" I repeated stupidly.

"My *bag*. With my *makeup* and stuff in it. You don't think I'm going to stick around this house, do you? I'm calling my dad to come and take me home! You guys can come, too," she added generously.

"What about the baby?" I asked in astonishment.

Pittsy folded her arms and just looked at me. "The *baby* can just take care of *himself* until the Grimms come home! I mean, he tried to *bite* me, after all!"

Well—it took me forever to persuade her not to leave Vaughn alone in the house. It took her even longer than that to agree that we needed to help the baby, not abandon him.

"He's only a baby," I kept saying. "He can't be

a full-fledged vampire yet. After all, he doesn't even have all his teeth! And look how cute and cuddly he acts most of the time."

"That's probably just an act," said Pittsy darkly.

"Yes, but Vincent acted like a vampire *all* the time. I know, I know," I said hastily. "I know you didn't think so. But the rest of us never saw the cute, cuddly side of him—that's for sure."

Trevor nodded in violent agreement.

"I think that what's happening is that Vaughn is turning into a vampire," I suggested. "And that's why we have to stop him. We can't let him grow up to be someone like Vincent!"

"Why not?" Pittsy said. "It's not our problem."

"It's not our problem if the whole world fills up with vampires because we wouldn't try to save a one-year-old baby? Would that be fair?" I asked. I didn't even care how goody-goodyish I sounded.

"Okay," Pittsy finally said in a grudging voice. "I guess you're right. But what do you think we should do, exactly? Call the police, or what?"

"I don't think that would work," I said. "I think we've got to take this into our own hands."

"Only no fighting vampires with our own hands," Trevor said anxiously.

"Oh, we wouldn't have to do anything like that," I promised him. "We'll use our brains."

Then I sighed. *What* brains? Mine certainly

wasn't trained in getting rid of vampires. I mean, we obviously hadn't done very well getting rid of Vincent. Trevor was so young that I probably couldn't count on him. And Pittsy—well, let's just say that I wasn't sure her brain was capable of figuring *anything* out.

Pittsy surprised me with her next question, though. "Meg, if all this is true, then how did it happen?" she asked. "Don't you have to be bitten by a vampire to turn into one?" She felt the bite marks on her own neck gingerly.

"You have to be bitten three times," I reminded her. "And Vaughnie doesn't even have all his teeth yet. Besides, we stopped him. So I don't think you're in any danger."

"Yeah, but how did *he* get bitten? Who would bite a baby?"

Now that was something I hadn't thought about.

"I did once take him to the old lighthouse where Vincent used to live," Pittsy confessed. "In his baby backpack."

"Why?" I asked in amazement. "That's a long walk! And to such a horrible spot, too!"

At least Pittsy had the grace to look embarrassed. "I just wanted to feel the memories—you know? Anyway, maybe he picked up some vampire germs there," she added quickly.

"Were there any bats?" I asked. "One of them might have bitten him." Pittsy said she didn't remember any bats. "And bats in the daytime would be the kind of thing I'd *notice*," she said.

"What about—I know this sounds stupid, but what about Vaughn's teething ring?" Trevor suggested timidly. "You know how no one knows where it came from, and how it looks just like that other ring—"

"Don't *remind* me," Pittsy said, moaning dramatically.

"And maybe if it's a vampire teething ring, then biting it might start turning Vaughn's teeth into vampire teeth," Trevor finished. "I'm prob'ly wrong, but—"

"*I* think you're probably right, Trev," I said, and I meant it. "Of course, we still don't know where the teething ring *came* from, but I bet you that's what's changing him."

"Let's go up and get that teething ring and flush it down the toilet!" Trevor suggested excitedly.

"We'd better wait," I said. "We need to plan things out a little bit first."

"It wouldn't be too great if the Grimms suddenly walked in and found us flushing away something of the baby's," Pittsy said. "They'd think we didn't respect his possessions or something. What time is it, anyway?"

We all turned to look at the wheezy grandfather clock in the hall. It was almost midnight.

"They'll be home soon," said Pittsy. "It's fine for you guys to be here—I told them you might be coming over. But let's finish up talking before they get back. After all, they might decide not to pay me if they find out that I think their baby is a vampire."

She rushed right on before I had time to react to that. "How do you un-vampire-ize a baby, anyway? You must have read how somewhere, Meg. You're such a big reader and everything."

She managed to make it sound like an insult, but I didn't have time to get mad. I wanted to get all this figured out before the Grimms came home.

"I don't really know," I said. "I think the best thing would be to train Vaughn to be a normal baby again."

"Housebreak him, you mean?" asked Trevor.

"He's not old enough for *that*," put in Pittsy. "Believe me."

I was thinking out loud. "Maybe if we could spend a big chunk of time with him," I said slowly, "we could kind of deprive him of all his vampire stuff—in a nice way, of course—and reintroduce him to regular baby stuff. I mean, we could take away his black clothes and dress him in pastels, and get him to eat something with garlic in it, and hide his toy bat somewhere—"

"And file down his teeth, I suppose," said Pittsy sarcastically.

"Do you have a better idea?" I asked.

"N-no," she admitted, "but *your* idea sounds awfully hard."

"I know. That's why we'd need to spend a big chunk of time with the baby. A whole day would be great, but I guess we can't have that."

"Hey, wait a minute!" said Pittsy. "We can! Next Saturday the Grimms are going to be *gone* for the whole day! They've got a wedding or something. I'm supposed to get here at eight in the morning, and they'll be home at around midnight that night. That should be enough time, don't you think?"

"It better be," I said. "Because after that, all my ideas will be used up."

Just then we heard the Grimms' car pull up in front of the house. The rest of our plans got lost in a flurry of bag-finding, snack-putting-away, waking up Trevor (he had suddenly dropped off to sleep right at the kitchen table), and relating a lot of confused reports to the Grimms on how Vaughnie had behaved.

Trevor and I had to sneak back into our house, of course, but that part was easy—at least compared to how hard it would have been to walk back home from the Grimms' house. The Grimms didn't ask what we were doing there, I was relieved to see. They were happy to give us a ride home and happy that we had been there to keep Pittsy company.

"I know our house can seem a little creepy at night," said Mr. Grimm with a chuckle.

Pittsy, Trevor, and I checked one another out. I was sure we were all thinking the same thing.

Creepy was hardly the word for this house. Not when a vampire was stalking through its halls. Not when a baby boy was about to become a bloodthirsty monster.

A bloodthirsty monster with the power to destroy the people closest to him—his own parents. And then go out in relentless search of other victims.

A bloodthirsty monster whom no one would ever, ever suspect was anything but an innocent child. . . .

CHAPTER TEN

"Meg, I've been thinking," said Trevor the next morning. He walked into my bedroom—I was reading in bed—and sat down on my desk chair.

"About what, Trev?" I asked.

Trevor lowered his voice to be sure Mom and Dad couldn't hear. "About Vaughn. Meg, what if he's not really turning into a vampire?"

"Then that would be good, wouldn't it?" I said abstractedly, turning a page in my book.

"But it's so mean to take away all a baby's favorite stuff if he's *not* really turning into a vampire! I'd hate it if I were a baby and someone did that to *me*!"

My brother did have a point. I put my book down and stared up at the ceiling.

"W-e-e-l-l," I said after a second, "his eyes did look awfully weird."

"Maybe that was just the lightning or something."

"And we have to remember that he *did* try to bite Pittsy in the neck," I said.

"Yeah, but maybe he just doesn't like her!" Trevor protested.

"Maybe. But even if he's *not* a vampire, Trev, it won't hurt him if we try to un-vampire-ize him. It might make him a little unhappy, but only for a day. And I think it would be much meaner if we didn't try to help him. I don't want to spend my whole life waiting around to see whether Vaughn's going to become a vampire. Not when we have a chance to save him."

In two days it would be Saturday. The Grimms would be away all day—and so, it turned out, would my parents. Mom and Dad were going on some horrible-sounding garden tour on the mainland. They were delighted to know that we'd be busy all day Saturday. Of course, they wouldn't have been if they knew what that something was. But I can't tell my parents *everything,* can I?

"Get it off me! Get it off me!" screamed Pittsy. Shrieking with rage, she stumbled to the sink and stuck her head under the faucet.

It was Saturday at last, and our first attempt to un-vampire-ize Vaughn was not turning out to be a total success.

True, baby oatmeal with garlic added wouldn't be *my* favorite food, either. But I had figured that maybe if I added enough cinnamon, it would disguise the taste enough to make Vaughn at least try it. "After all," I'd reasoned, "if garlic wards off vampires, *eating* garlic might cancel out the vampire in Vaughn."

My reasoning might have been right, but we weren't going to get the chance to find out. At the first whiff of his oatmeal Vaughn took the bowl and dumped it over Pittsy's head. He had good aim, for a one-year-old.

"I guess I was wrong," I said sheepishly. "Here, let me help you, Kelly. There's some on the back of your neck."

"You and your brilliant ideas," Pittsy sputtered from under the faucet. "*You* get to be the guinea pig in the next experiment."

Vaughn, watching from his high chair, suddenly laughed. "Yeah, big joke," grumbled Pittsy as she reached for a dishtowel to dry her hair.

"What *is* our next experiment, Meg?" Trevor asked brightly.

"Dressing the baby, I guess," I said. (He was still in his black nightshirt.) "Why don't you run upstairs and take all the black clothes out of his dresser? Just hide them somewhere so he won't be able to pick them."

I turned to the baby, who was now happily eating the bowl of tomato soup he had wanted all along. His face was smeared with gruesome blobs of red.

"Okay, Vaughn-O," I said. "Let's clean that blood—I mean, ketchup—off you and get you into some nice, babyish, pale blue and yellow clothes."

"*You* clean him off," said Pittsy ungraciously.

I did the best I could, and we lugged him upstairs to his room. Trevor had done a good job. He had left Vaughn's dresser drawers open to reveal neatly folded stacks of sunsuits and sleepers—all pastel. There wasn't a patch of black in sight.

"Let's go, honey," said Pittsy cheerfully. (The subject of clothes—anybody's clothes—always cheered her up.) She took Vaughn from my arms and led him over to the dresser. "What would you like to wear today?"

Eagerly the baby reached toward the neatly arranged piles of clothes. He riffled through the first pile like a squirrel going for an acorn in leaves.

No black. Vaughn pitched the pile of clothes onto the floor and moved swiftly to the next pile. His hands were moving faster now. When he discovered that there was no black in that stack of clothes, either, he made a little growling sound in the back of his throat. The second pile of clothes hit the floor.

On to the next pile while the three of us watched in amazement. Vaughn's hands were a blur, and he was starting to emit a high-pitched whine like the buzz of a circular saw. No black! He picked up the stack and hurled it against the wall.

"What an arm!" marveled Trevor. "He's going to be a great pitcher when he grows up."

A vampire pitcher? There were fuzzy pastel clothes everywhere now. Vaughn's face was purple with frustration.

He ripped through the last pile in the drawer at blinding speed. Still he found no black.

"EEEEEEEEEEEEEYAAAAAAAH!" he screamed in a rage—and yanked the whole drawer out of the dresser. He threw himself down on top of it and began pounding so hard the wood started to splinter.

"All right, that's enough," I said grimly. "Where's his black stuff, Trevor?"

"Under the crib," my brother told me. "But you said—"

"I take it back. We can't let him tear the house down."

I dashed to the crib, grabbed a handful of black clothes, and held them out to the baby.

"Are these what you're looking for?" I asked him.

Instant silence. Vaughn sat up, smiled at me, and gave my face a little pat.

"A-ba-ba-ba-ba," he said sweetly.

A pair of black sweatpants, one black T-shirt, one black sock with red spots and one black sock with green stripes, one black bib, and one black ski hat later, Vaughn was finally wearing an outfit he liked.

I won't describe everything else we went through trying to change Vaughn back into a regular baby. Why dwell on all the failures of that long, long day?

Let me just mention that when we offered him a nice teddy bear instead of the rubber bat he wanted, Vaughn pulled the nice teddy bear's head right off his nice shoulders. When we tried to switch from "Sesame Street" to a cartoon show, Vaughn grabbed the remote control from Pittsy's hand and hurled it out the window. When we tried to put him down for a nap without his teething ring, he held his breath until he turned blue, then spit up all over my hand.

When I tried to change his diaper, he cried, but that was only because he was so tired. (He had refused to take a nap after we tried to take away his teething ring.)

"Poor baby," I crooned as I fastened the tapes on his diaper. "You've had quite a day, haven't you? Let's give you some supper and then have a bath."

After a light, messy supper in which a ketchup sandwich and strawberry jelly joined lunch's tomato soup in Vaughn's hair, he was even more ready for a bath. "I'll do the dishes if you'll bathe him," Pittsy offered. "I could *really, really* use a break."

"I'll help you, Meg," Trevor said. "He doesn't use black soap, does he?"

No, and he didn't bathe in blood, either. In fact, giving Vaughn a bath was just like giving one to a regular baby. He shouted and splashed and poured water out onto the floor, and I had more fun than I'd had all day.

"Don't you have to brush his teeth?" Trevor asked as I was getting Vaughn into his lovely black sleeper.

I paused. "I don't think most one-year-olds have their teeth brushed," I said. "Anyway, *I'm* not brushing those little points. It won't hurt to skip one day."

Maybe it was his unbrushed teeth that kept Vaughn awake. He'd had such a long day that I expected him to fall asleep right away. Unfortunately, he seemed determined to make the day even longer. The minute I closed his bedroom door and tiptoed away, he started chattering to himself. Another minute after that, and he was whimpering. Another minute after *that*, and he had reached full bellowing mode.

I staggered downstairs and collapsed on a chair in the den, where Pittsy was watching videos on TV. "Your turn," I gasped. "I can't face him again."

"Oh, like *I* can," Pittsy grumped, without moving.

"Come on," I begged. "I've been with him for the last hour!"

"Okay. Okay." Pittsy was still staring at the TV. "I'll go up right when this video is over. I promise."

"Let me just see what the next song is," she said when that video was done. "Oh, I love this one. I'll go up in one second, I promise."

"Never mind," I said with a sigh. "I'll do it."

"Thanks, Meg," said Pittsy. "That's really sweet of you."

Trevor came up to help me, but there was nothing either of us could do to cheer Vaughn up. He didn't want a bottle, but he didn't want to let go of his bottle, either. He didn't want to be rocked, but he didn't want me to put him down. He didn't want Trevor to play peekaboo, but he didn't want Trevor to go downstairs.

"He doesn't want *anything,*" I finally said in despair. "He only wants to cry."

I glanced wearily at my watch. It was eight-thirty—Trevor's bedtime. "Wouldn't you like to lie down on the Grimms' bed for a while?" I asked over the baby's wails. "*One* of us may as well get some sleep, at least."

Trevor yawned. "I *am* tired," he admitted. "Will you get me up if you need me?"

"Absolutely." I took him into the Grimms' room and covered him with their quilt. He was asleep before I'd switched off the light.

I carried Vaughn downstairs and into the den, hoping to get him to have his bottle in front of the TV. Pittsy glanced up at us irritably as we came in.

"Do you *mind,* Meg?" she asked. "I can't hear the TV with all that squawking."

"Fine!" I snapped. "I'll take him outside! Would that be better for you?"

Pittsy didn't seem to notice my tone. "That'd be great," she said. "He could probably use some fresh air. And so could you. You look kind of gray."

Without another word I picked up the baby, bottle and all, and stalked out of the house.

I paused outside the front door to take a deep breath. It was the first time I'd been outside all day, and I suddenly realized how cooped up I'd been feeling. The night air seemed new and cool.

Insects buzzed in the trees, and from behind the house I could hear waves frothing along the beach. In the blue light of the full moon everything I saw was sharp edged but shadowy at the same time. It was a wonderful change from the stale, rumpled, TV-tainted atmosphere inside the house.

The baby seemed to feel the difference, too. He relaxed and fell silent in my arms, looking around alertly.

"Want to take a little walk, Vaughnie?" I asked softly. I set him down on the ground. With a little coo of happiness he began to toddle forward into the darkness, still clutching his bottle.

"Not too far," I warned, taking his hand. "We need to stay close to the house."

Now the baby was tugging eagerly on my hand, pulling me down the front path. "Sah? Sah?" he asked eagerly, gesturing in front of him.

"What are you asking about?" I stopped and heard the splash of the water in the fountain.

"Oh, did you say 'what's that'? That's the fountain we hear," I said. "We can't play in it now, though. It's too—"

"Fahn-tah!" Vaughn chirped.

"That's right! *Fountain!* Good for—"

"Fahn-tah!" he repeated proudly. He pulled his hand out of mine, toddling as fast as he could into the darkness toward the fountain.

"Wait, Vaughn!" I called, racing after him. "It's too dark out there! You'll—"

Too late.

Just as I reached him, the baby tripped over a stone lying in front of the fountain. He flew forward, and his mouth struck the stone edge of the fountain.

A thin trickle of blood flowed from Vaughn's lip into the moonlit water.

"Oh, Vaughn! Are you all right?" I raced forward and picked him up. He was crying, but not too hard, and I could see that his lip wasn't badly cut.

"Thank heaven!" I gasped, giving him a hug. "Boy, I was scared for a second. You could have really hurt yourself—"

A rumbling sound, like that of a distant avalanche, interrupted me.

I glanced up, still cradling the baby in my arms—and froze in terror.

The statue was moving. This time there was no doubt about it.

It was definitely not my imagination. The statue was stretching its arms as though after a long sleep, and as its arms moved, the stone binding them began to crack.

Now it turned its head toward me, and I saw the horrible stone face begin to transform itself into a living face. The blind stone eyes darkened and fixed themselves on me. The gray stone skin smoothed itself into flesh that was just as gray. The lips darkened to a deep red and curled into a soundless snarl.

The legs hadn't started to change. They were still solid stone. But I recognized the face now.

It was a face I knew all too well—the vampire face of Vincent Graver.

"You're—you're inside the statue!" I gasped.

"That is correct, Meg," he answered in his cold, dead voice.

Then he bent down and plucked the baby out of my arms like a flower.

CHAPTER ELEVEN

"Da-da!" said Vaughn happily, reaching up to pat Vincent's gray face.

"No, Vaughn," I whimpered. "That's not your daddy."

"Da-da!" the baby insisted. He snuggled cozily down in the shelter of Vincent's cape (what used to be wings when he was a statue) and started sucking on his bottle.

"The child is very comfortable with me, as you can see," said Vincent. "No, Vaughn. I do not care for any milk, thank you. He does not know it yet, but we are closely related."

I had forgotten how much I hated that slow, dead, formal, lumbering voice. "No one's related to *you*, Vincent," I snapped. "Corpses don't have relatives."

"I have warned you before about that tongue of yours, Meg," Vincent replied icily. A cloud slid past the moon and disappeared. "I see you still have not profited by my advice. But it surprises

me that you would attempt to insult me while I am holding a child in your charge."

That shut me up. No matter what happened to me, I couldn't let anything happen to Vaughn.

"I-I apologize, Vincent," I said in a shaky voice. "I won't let it happen again."

"An apology from Meg Swain! What a refreshing change!" commented Vincent. He folded the baby closer in his cape and stared at me.

I stared back. I couldn't help it. From the waist up Vincent was—well, Vincent. From the waist down he was still made of stone.

"How did you get in there?" I heard myself asking.

Vincent bowed slightly. "An intelligent question, for once. I shall answer it."

Good, I thought. *Keep him talking as long as you can.* That's what they always do with the criminal in detective stories, isn't it? Not that I had any guarantee it would work in real life, but there was nothing else to try. . . .

"Your two prior attempts to remove me from this earth were quite successful, Meg," said Vincent. "Under normal conditions it would be some time before I could return to life in corporeal form."

Thank heaven.

"However, vampires in my family—for I *do*

have relatives, many of them—are given a third chance to inhabit the world by first inhabiting an appropriate inanimate object."

"Like that statue," I said, thinking privately that compared to Vincent, the statue was about as frightening as Bambi.

"Like this statue," Vincent agreed. "And so I returned to earth within this stone form. And waited to see whether my chance would come to escape."

"But—but how did you get *out*?" I asked.

"There are certain conditions that need to be met. One is a full moon." The moon was staring down at us now. I wondered how I could have been happy to step out into a night like this.

"Another condition," Vincent continued, "is a drop of vampire blood. No, Vaughn. Do not pull my collar. This condition, too, was met."

"What do you mean?" I asked, bewildered.

"The inanimate form—in this case, the statue—must come into contact with a drop of vampire blood in order to become animated," Vincent explained.

"But that didn't happen!" I objected.

Vincent glanced down at Vaughn, who was now holding his bottle with one hand and plucking Vincent's cape with the other.

"You are a careless babysitter, Meg," Vincent

said. "Have you not learned that when you let a baby out of your sight, all kinds of accidents can happen?"

"But I didn't mean to—" Then the meaning of Vincent's words sank in. "You mean when Vaughn cut his lip on the fountain? *That* was what did it?"

Vincent nodded.

"No!" I cried wildly. "Vaughn's not a vampire!"

"Not yet. But he is well on the way to becoming one."

"Then I was right," I whispered.

At that moment, though, Vaughn looked less like a vampire than ever. He had twined his chubby arms around Vincent's neck and was nestling his cheek against Vincent's.

"You were right." Vincent patted the baby's head stiffly. I could tell he had never done it before. "I can still summon up my brethren when I need them. The mere act of thinking about them sends a powerful message that they cannot fail to receive.

"And so I summoned a cousin of mine in the old country and asked him to send the teething ring so Vaughn might be started on the vampire path. The post office is a helpful, though unwitting, vampire aid."

Suddenly I remembered the box I'd stumbled

over on my first visit to the Grimms'. The box that said "For Dear Baby" in spiky, old-fashioned handwriting—the box whose sender Mrs. Grimm had never identified. That box must have contained the teething ring.

"But why Vaughn?" I asked indignantly. "He's never done anything to you!"

"No, but that is no concern of mine. Although it was certainly a pleasant coincidence to find that in a house as attractive as this, with a statue as convenient as this, lived a child whose initials are the same as mine. Fate must have been on my side.

"What I was concerned with was revenge—revenge on *you.*" Vincent glared evilly at me. "Revenge on your meddling insolence, Meg. You should never have gotten in the way of my plans to—let us say—convert this island."

"To change us all into vampires, you mean," I said bitterly. "What kind of person *wouldn't* get in the way of plans like that?"

"A very smart person, I should say," Vincent remarked. And the ominous note in his voice made me feel sick with fear.

"Ga-BAH!" Vaughn added, waving his bottle around for emphasis. "Da-da."

Quickly, hoping to distract Vincent further, I asked, "Why a teething ring? It seems like a kind of roundabout way of turning someone into a vampire."

"It is not an ordinary teething ring," replied Vincent, as though I hadn't already known *that*. "It was carved from the bone of a vampire skeleton."

"I thought vampires crumbled when they were—uh—used up," I said. "I didn't know they ever left skeletons."

"In very rare cases—during severe epidemics, for example—an occasional elderly vampire will cease to live without losing his body," Vincent explained. "We always save the bones. They are used for the express purpose of changing mortal babies into vampires."

"Gross!" I squealed before I could stop myself. "Then Vaughn has been chewing on a *dead vampire*?"

"I do not care for your tone," Vincent said, "but, yes. He has gradually absorbed the vampire essence into his own small body."

"Forever?" I asked quickly. There might still be hope for Vaughn, if I could get him away from Vincent. . . .

"Forever," Vincent replied. "Once the absorption process is completed. And I have no doubt it *will* be completed before long."

"Just as a matter of curiosity," I said, "is there

anything that could destroy you permanently? Not that I expect that to happen," I added politely. "I'm wondering, that's all."

"You do have some intelligence, I see," replied my former babysitter. "The bite of another vampire could incapacitate me for an indefinite length of time. But that is a most unlikely fate, I would say."

"And—uh—one other question," I babbled. "Those bats in my attic the other night—were those—"

"Friends of mine, yes. Occasionally I summon them to keep me company. I merely asked them to send you a warning. But I should have known you would not heed me. Indeed, your brother was the only person in your household to notice the visitors. I have always considered him more intelligent than you."

I noticed, suddenly, that the insects had stopped chirping. Dead silence surrounded us, except for the hissing of the waves and the fountain's mocking splash. With one corner of my brain I hoped Vaughn wouldn't get wet. It was too cold for that.

"Kelly Pitts is the child's babysitter, as you know," Vincent's dead voice broke into my thoughts. "During my . . . relationship with Kelly, I managed to bite her twice. All she needs to become a vampire is a third bite."

Yes, I know that, too.

"For this reason, Vaughn seemed the ideal subject," Vincent went on. "He is small enough that the conversion process would have been easy. He could have started his career with Kelly, and then proceeded to turn other trusting souls into vampires as he grew older. By then, of course, Kelly, too, would have joined me in the vampire kingdom."

That same distant corner of my brain wondered why Vincent kept saying "could" and "would." Hadn't he just been insisting that this was all about to happen? Why did he sound so doubtful now?

"You interfered with my plans, Meg." It was almost as though Vincent had read my mind. "I cannot complete my own transformation process without moving things along more quickly. So I must change my plans a little.

"And I will start with this infant."

Vincent stared down at Vaughn, who was smiling up at him. A cold, dead smile flickered across Vincent's gray features, and for a brief second his eyes sparked to life.

Then he lowered his head to sink his teeth into Vaughn's neck.

CHAPTER TWELVE

I stood there, transfixed with horror. I didn't even scream. What good would it do? Everything was over now. A scream would only frighten the baby when there was nothing anyone could do to help him.

Vincent's teeth were gleaming in the moonlight. Long, curved, and deadly sharp, they were more frightening than any animal's I had ever seen. They were just about to pierce the baby's tender skin. . . .

"Hey, what's the matter with the fountain?" came a voice from behind me.

It was Pittsy with my brother right behind her.

"Vincent!" Trevor gasped.

Startled, Vincent raised his head.

"*Vincent!* You cheating scab! What are you doing here?" Pittsy yelled. She didn't even seem to wonder how Vincent could be alive again or to notice that he was still stone from the waist down. "After everything you've done to me, you come back to apologize? Well, no way will I forgive you." Pittsy drew herself up haughtily. "I'm a very, very sensitive person, and . . ."

Then, at last, she saw Vaughn. "Hey! Put that baby down!" she ordered. "Do you want to get me into trouble with the Grimms on top of everything *else* you've done to me?"

"Be silent, Kelly!" Vincent thundered. "Your chatter sickens me!"

That was the point when Vaughn suddenly decided he wasn't happy in Vincent's arms after all. He began to cry. Arching his back in that maddening way babies have, he starting flailing around and hitting Vincent in the chest with his bottle.

"Meg, help him!" Trevor wailed.

"I don't know how," I said, calm with despair.

"Now see what you've done," Vincent told Pittsy angrily. He gripped the wailing, thrashing baby more firmly, trying to get a good bitehold.

Anyone who *knows* anything about babies could tell you that they don't like being squeezed, and anyone who knows about babies also knows how slippery they can be when they want you to put them down. Vincent, I could see, knew neither of those things. He just wasn't used to holding an angry toddler. Vaughn, of course, was not especially interested in holding still so that Vincent could bite his neck.

"Ruination!" Vincent muttered under his breath as he struggled to find the baby's neck with his teeth.

"Now you know how *I* feel," Pittsy remarked, so unexpectedly that Vincent, Trevor, and I all turned to her in amazement. "Taking care of kids is really, really hard. You have to—"

At that moment a cloud slid across the moon again. For a second the night became pitch-black. I realized for that second Vincent lost his power to free himself from the statue. There had to be a full moon, he had said. . . .

This was my only moment to act. I darted forward in the darkness and grabbed the baby from Vincent's hands.

"Pittsy!" I screamed, holding the baby out at arm's length. "Take him!"

I shoved Vaughn forward. The next second I felt Pittsy's outstretched hands fumbling over mine. Then she was pulling the baby safely out of reach.

"Ouch!" Pittsy complained. "I broke a nail. And *what* did you call me, Meg?"

The moon emerged from its cloud cover and heartlessly lit up the landscape again.

Even if I had wanted to answer Pittsy, I couldn't have. Vincent's hands had just closed around my throat.

Vincent switched his grip to my shoulders and slowly, slowly began to pull me up toward him. Out of the corner of my eye I could see that the stone half of his body was starting to ripple. He would be stepping free of his prison as soon as he had bitten me. And then Pittsy and the baby and I—and Trevor, and perhaps the whole island—would fall under his deadly power. . . .

My neck was almost level with those deadly teeth now. Vincent smiled horribly at me, and I saw that the pupils of his eyes were blazing red.

"Welcome to the other side," he said softly. "Three bites is all it takes. . . ." He aimed his pointed teeth right at my throat.

Just then Vaughn wriggled loose from Pittsy's arms. Squawking with indignation, he toddled swiftly toward the fountain.

"Nuh-nuh-nuh-nuh-*nuh*!" he shouted.

"You are all such idiots. Even this child." Vincent gave a hollow laugh. Still holding my throat with one strong hand, he bent down to scoop up the baby with the other.

"Bad," said the baby clearly and sank his teeth into Vincent's outstretched hand.

"Hey, you said that really great!" said Pittsy, paying attention to the least important thing, as usual.

"That's right, Vaughn! Sic 'em!" my brother shouted proudly. "At least we can die like heroes!"

Vincent let out a howl of anguish and shook the baby loose. Trevor darted forward and grabbed Vaughn again, pulling him safely out of reach this time.

"NO!" Vincent bellowed, shaking his head blindly back and forth. "The bite of another vampire . . ."

In his pain he dropped me into the fountain. I started to flounder away through the water, but Vincent grabbed me again.

"I can still destroy you, Meg Swain," he hissed.

His hands were clutching my throat so hard I couldn't breathe. Blackness swirled in front of my eyes, and I felt my knees start to buckle.

Then a terrible weight pressed down on me, and Vincent's chilling grip became deathly cold.

His arms had turned back to stone.

Struggling to breathe, I looked up just in time to see Vincent's face freeze in a snarl of agony. His mouth was open as if he were shouting, but no sound came out. The transformation back to stone was complete.

And I was trapped in the strangling arms of a stone statue.

I closed my eyes and waited for unconsciousness to overtake me. Hundreds of pounds of stone pressed down on me with unbearable weight.

Then, there came a rumbling like that of a distant avalanche—and I was free.

How?

I stepped back, bewildered, and scrambled out of the fountain as fast as I could.

With a wrenching crack the stone statue collapsed before my eyes and crumbled to pieces at the bottom of the fountain.

CHAPTER THIRTEEN

The three of us didn't wait to see what happened next. We dashed inside with the baby and bolted the front door behind us.

"Upstairs," I gasped. "The baby's room. He won't see us there."

Not that there was anyone left *to* see us, but you know what I mean. We thundered up the stairs into Vaughn's room and slammed his door.

"Oh, my God," Pittsy said, collapsing into a chair. "That was the most—I was never so scared in my— Is the baby okay?"

She held Vaughn out at arm's length to examine him. He was screaming full-volume, but we were used to that. It's perfectly normal for one-year-olds who've been manhandled by vampires to get a little tearful.

"It's okay, Vaughnie," Pittsy crooned, rocking him back and forth. "You're fine now."

As the baby's shrieks began to quiet, Pittsy turned to me and said, "If you guys wouldn't mind making him a bottle, I'll give it to him and try getting him to go to sleep." She stared down at her knees, blinking hard. "I felt—I felt pretty awful when I saw Vincent holding him. I know I can't make it up to him, but I want to try.

"After all, Vaughn is terribly, terribly sensitive, just like me," she added. "It *takes* a sensitive person to understand another sensitive person, you know."

"I know," I said with a grin and headed downstairs with Trevor to make a bottle. I'd never be able to get used to a *totally* nice Pittsy, anyway.

About twenty minutes later, after Pittsy had given Trevor his bottle and put him to sleep, she came tiptoeing downstairs and found me in the kitchen, where I had made some hot chocolate and cinnamon toast for all of us.

"I thought we could use a little comfort food," I said.

"Perfect." Pittsy sat down and sighed with relief. "Vaughn calmed down right away. I think he'll sleep now. And look, I brought this down with me—" She showed me the teething ring. "He was too tired to notice when I took it away. What do you think I should do with it?"

"Gee, I don't know. Do you think it's still dangerous?"

"I sure wouldn't want to take any chances on

it. Let's burn it up," Pittsy suggested. "We can just drop it into one of the burners. I'm glad the Grimms have a gas stove."

"But we might ruin the stove," I objected.

"Who cares? The Grimms are remodeling, anyway, aren't they? At least you can hold it over the flame and kind of—you know—sterilize it. Maybe it will melt into a lump."

"But it's made of bone. Bone doesn't melt," I pointed out.

"Oh, come on," said Pittsy impatiently. "You act as though I'm trying to burn the house down. Let me just *try*, anyway. It can't *hurt* anything."

She picked up the teething ring on a fork, turned up the burner flame as high as she could, and gingerly held the ring over the fire.

A dark green flame shot up to the ceiling.

"Uh-oh," Pittsy said. "Guess I was wrong."

"Quick, turn it off!" I said, leaping to my feet. But before I could reach the stove, a coil of foul-smelling green smoke uncurled itself into the room.

From far away I thought I heard a moan, as if someone were in pain.

Then the red stone melted like butter, and the ring became a pile of ash.

I stared down at the ring's remains. "That's *it*?" I asked.

Pittsy seemed to be a little startled, too. "I-I guess so."

I could hardly believe that such a dangerous toy could have been destroyed so quickly. Were its powers really gone forever?

Well, it was no use trying to figure *that* out. I put on some oven mitts and whisked the burner pan into the sink. I squirted about a quart of detergent over it and then turned on the water full-blast.

"We'll let it soak overnight," I said when I'd switched off the tap. "That will take care of any extra, um, stains."

Pittsy shuddered. "I hope it will take care of *Vincent,* too. What happened before I got out there, anyway?"

When I'd finished describing the scene by the fountain, Pittsy and Trevor were both pale. "You don't—you don't think he'll—you know—pull himself back together, do you?" Pittsy asked.

"I don't think he can," I answered. "He said that the bite of another vampire was the only thing that could destroy him permanently."

"Was that what he was talking about?" inquired my brother. "I didn't get it. But I thought Vaughn was just turning into a vampire. He's not one, is he—not a whole one?"

"Not yet. Vincent said the transformation wasn't complete."

"So it might *not* have been the bite that crumbled Vincent up," said Trevor. "I mean, if Vaughn isn't a vampire . . ."

The question hung in the air, and I couldn't answer it. At last I said, "Well, at least something destroyed him. We should be glad of that."

"Oh, I am, I am," Pittsy said fervently, and Trevor nodded with equal fervor.

Under her breath Pittsy added, "I just hope it lasts."

"What on earth happened to the fountain?" Mrs. Grimm asked us a couple of hours later.

"You know, it was the strangest thing," Pittsy said without missing a beat. "The three of us were sitting in the den when we heard this cracking noise. We ran outside, and the whole thing had just, like, crumbled away! I would have thought it was like struck by lightning, except there *wasn't* any lightning. It was super-weird. But we'll replace it if you want us to, since it happened while we were in charge."

I was glad neither of the Grimms called her bluff. (How do three kids go about replacing a *statue*?) Instead, Mrs. Grimm said, "Oh, no, don't be silly. I'm glad nature stepped in and saved us the trouble. I always hated that statue. It gave me the creeps."

We eyed one another in silent agreement.

"And Vaughnie was fine?" asked Mr. Grimm.

"He was just great," said Pittsy proudly. "He kept us on the go all day long. He's such a brave little kid—I mean, so *energetic.*"

"Wonderful," said Mrs. Grimm, fishing in her purse for her wallet. "I hate to ask it, Kelly, but are you by any chance free tomorrow afternoon? There's an auction we'd like to pop in and see if we could. But of course I'll understand if you want a break from sitting."

"No! I'd love to come!" said Pittsy.

As we all walked out of the house toward the Grimms' car, she whispered to me, "It'll give me a chance to see whether Vaughn's been un-vampire-ized yet."

"Hello, Meg? It's Kelly. I'm calling from the Grimms' house."

"Hi, Kelly! How's Vaughn doing?"

"He's fantastic," Pittsy said happily. "He picked a blue sunsuit and orange socks and a red hat and one other yellow sock to wear today. I mean, he has no fashion sense, but at least he didn't want to wear any black. And he *walked away* when the Count was on 'Sesame Street.' And he threw his rubber bat out the window. And guess what he's eating right now? Some leftover garlic bread."

* * *

The rest of the summer passed pretty quickly after that. One day I walked to the Grimms' house to meet Pittsy and saw a man shoveling the remnants of the stone statue into a pickup truck.

"Where are you taking that?" I asked.

He looked at me as though I were crazy. "To the dump, where else? Do you want it for anything?"

I stared at the pile of crumbled stone in the back of the truck. In one corner I thought I recognized part of a clawed hand. And surely that chip of stone was a pointed tooth. . . .

I shook my head. "No," I said. "I don't want it for anything."

Good-bye, Vincent. Enjoy your new home.

"Meg, have you seen my binoculars?"

"Hey, Dad! Do you want to pack these flip-flops, or should I just toss 'em?"

"Honey, do you remember how to turn off the water?"

"Where on earth is Pooch? Honestly, that cat makes me insane! Why does he *always* disappear at times like this?"

It's such fun packing to go home from vacation, isn't it?

As I stared around our living room, which was filled with open, gaping suitcases and wet beach towels, I could hardly believe the summer was really over. Tomorrow, we'd be back in Delaware. A week later we'd be in school, and Vincent would just seem like a bad dream. I would sit in math class going over the summer in my mind and wondering whether I'd just imagined the whole thing. Then Mr. Sherbinski would call on me, and I wouldn't know what he was talking about.

I chuckled to myself. "Gee, Vincent," I wanted to say, "you're *still* getting me in trouble."

On the coffee table there was big stack of library books that needed to go back to the Moose Island Public Library before we left. I picked them up and headed out to the car with them. If this summer was like previous ones, we'd forget all about those library books until we were home with them. I guess that's a Swain family tradition, too.

As I piled the books onto the front seat of the car, I saw a quick flicker of movement beside me. "Pooch! You're back!" I exclaimed. I turned to grab him—

And saw the corner of a black cape disappearing around the side of the house.

"*No,*" I whispered. "It's not possible."

Suddenly the air seemed very cold. A moaning wind rose up and rustled the trees around me. I thought I heard a faint whisper hovering just overhead.

"I shall never return to Moose Island, Meg, but I am not done with you."

It was Vincent's voice, of course.

Of course I convinced myself it hadn't been real. There was no way a stone statue could reconstruct itself. Vincent had been destroyed by the baby he'd tried to destroy, and he wasn't going to come back for a long time. *Maybe he'll never be back!* I told myself optimistically. *Nothing lasts forever, not even vampires.*

In the flurry of last-minute packing (we forgot to get the library books back, as usual) and saying good-bye (I was amazed to realize I would miss Pittsy), I forced myself to stop thinking about Vincent. Once we were on the ferry, I actually succeeded.

It was a beautiful day for traveling. As the ferry cut merrily through the water, Trevor and I stood against the railing and threw popcorn to the sea gulls. "Rats with wings," Mom always calls sea gulls, but I like them. This would be our last chance to feed them for a whole year.

"Look at that one, Trev!" I called. "He's huge! He can hardly fly!"

An especially fat sea gull labored through the air toward the boat. I tossed him some popcorn, but he missed. Squawking with frustration, he flapped down toward the water, where the popcorn was now floating.

I leaned over the railing to watch his progress. He flew clumsily down to the water, dipped down to grab some popcorn in his beak, and struggled away with it.

There was my reflection, staring up at me. I gave myself a cheery wave, and my reflection waved back at me.

Who was that standing next to my reflection?

A tall, dark, motionless figure with a flapping cape . . .

I straightened up in a panic and glanced around. No, no one was standing next to me except my brother, and he wasn't tall enough to cast a reflection.

But down in the water the dark image of Vincent Graver was traveling along with the ferry. And for the rest of the ride, that image never left us.

ANN HODGMAN is a former children's book editor and the author of over twenty-five children's books, including the popular *My Babysitter Is a Vampire, My Babysitter Has Fangs*, and *My Babysitter Bites Again*. In addition to humorous fiction for children, she has written teen mysteries and non-fiction for reluctant readers. She is also a writer for *The Big Picture*, a series of educational posters distributed in schools nationwide.

JOHN PIERARD has illustrated the bestselling My Teacher is an Alien series and the My Babysitter is a Vampire series. His pictures can also be found in several books in the Time Machine series and in *Isaac Asimov's Science Fiction Magazine*. He lives in Manhattan.